THE

ſUMMER

BOOK

Also by Tove Jansson

Sun City

FOR CHILDREN

Moominsummer Madness
Moominland Midwinter
Tales from Moominvalley
Finn Family Moomintroll
Exploits of Moominpappa
Moominpappa at Sea
Moomin, Mymble, and Little My
Comet in Moominland
Who Will Comfort Toffle
Moominvalley in November
The Dangerous Journey
The Sculptor's Daughter

THE

∫UMMER

BOOK

TOVE JANSSON

Translated from the Swedish by Thomas Teal

SCHOCKEN BOOKS   NEW YORK

Library of Congress Cataloging in Publication Data

Jansson, Tove.
  The summer book.

  Translation of: Sommarboken.
  Reprint. Originally published: 1st American ed.
New York: Pantheon Books, 1975, © 1974
  I. Title.
PT9875.J37S613 1988   839.7'374   87-42995
ISBN 0-8052-0850-X (pbk.)

Manufactured in the United States of America

First Schocken Paperback Edition

THE
SUMMER
BOOK

The Morning Swim

IT WAS AN EARLY, very warm morning in July, and it had rained during the night. The bare granite steamed, the moss and crevices were drenched with moisture, and all the colors everywhere had deepened. Below the veranda, the vegetation in the morning shade was like a rain forest of lush, evil leaves and flowers, which she had to be careful not to break as she searched. She held one hand in front of her mouth and was constantly afraid of losing her balance.

"What are you doing?" asked little Sophia.

"Nothing," her grandmother answered. "That is to say," she added angrily, "I'm looking for my false teeth."

The child came down from the veranda. "Where did you lose them?" she asked.

"Here," said her grandmother. "I was standing right there and they fell somewhere in the peonies." They looked together.

"Let me," Sophia said. "You can hardly walk. Move over."

She dived beneath the flowering roof of the garden and crept among green stalks and stems. It was pretty and mysterious down on the soft black earth. And there were the teeth, white and pink, a whole mouthful of old teeth. "I've got them!" the child cried, and stood up. "Put them in."

"But you can't watch," Grandmother said. "That's private."

Sophia held the teeth behind her back.

"I want to watch," she said.

So Grandmother put the teeth in, with a smacking noise. They went in very easily. It had really hardly been worth mentioning.

"When are you going to die?" the child asked.

And Grandmother answered, "Soon. But that is not the least concern of yours."

"Why?" her grandchild asked.

She didn't answer. She walked out on the rock and on toward the ravine.

"We're not allowed out there!" Sophia screamed.

"I know," the old woman answered disdainfully. "Your father won't let either one of us go out to the ravine, but we're going anyway, because your father is asleep and he won't know."

They walked across the granite. The moss was slippery. The sun had come up a good way now, and everything was steaming. The whole island was covered with a bright haze. It was very pretty.

"Will they dig a hole?" asked the child amiably.

"Yes," she said. "A big hole." And she added, insidiously, "Big enough for all of us."

"How come?" the child asked.

They walked on toward the point.

"I've never been this far before," Sophia said. "Have you?"

"No," her grandmother said.

They walked all the way out onto the little promontory, where the rock descended into the water in terraces that became fainter and fainter until there was total darkness. Each step down was edged with a light green seaweed fringe that swayed back and forth with the movement of the sea.

"I want to go swimming," the child said. She waited for opposition, but none came. So she took off her clothes, slowly and nervously. She glanced at her grandmother—you can't depend on people who just let things happen. She put her legs in the water.

"It's cold," she said.

"Of course it's cold," the old woman said, her thoughts somewhere else. "What did you expect?"

The child slid in up to her waist and waited anxiously.

"Swim," her grandmother said. "You can swim."

It's deep, Sophia thought. She forgets I've never swum in deep water unless somebody was with me. And she climbed out again and sat down on the rock.

"It's going to be a nice day today," she declared.

The sun had climbed higher. The whole island, and the sea, were glistening. The air seemed very light.

"I can dive," Sophia said. "Do you know what it feels like when you dive?"

"Of course I do," her grandmother said. "You let go of everything and get ready and just dive. You can feel the seaweed against your legs. It's brown, and the water's clear, lighter toward the top, with lots of bubbles. And you glide. You hold your breath and glide and turn and come up, let yourself rise and breathe out. And then you float. Just float."

"And all the time with your eyes open," Sophia said.

"Naturally. People don't dive with their eyes shut."

"Do you believe I can dive without me showing you?" the child asked.

"Yes, of course," Grandmother said. "Now get dressed. We can get back before he wakes up."

The first weariness came closer. When we get

home, she thought, when we get back I think I'll
take a little nap. And I must remember to tell him
this child is still afraid of deep water.

Moonlight

ONE TIME in April there was a full moon, and the
sea was covered with ice. Sophia woke up and remembered that they had come back to the island
and that she had a bed to herself because her
mother was dead. The fire was still burning in the
stove, and the flames flickered on the ceiling, where
the boots were hung up to dry. She climbed down
to the floor, which was very cold, and looked out
through the window.

The ice was black, and in the middle of the ice
she saw the open stove door and the fire—in fact
she saw two stove doors, very close together. In the
second window, the two fires were burning under-
ground, and through the third window she saw a
double reflection of the whole room, trunks and
chests and boxes with gaping lids. They were filled
with moss and snow and dry grass, all of them
open, with bottoms of coal-black shadow. She saw
two children out on the rock, and there was a rowan

tree growing right through them. The sky behind them was dark blue.

She lay down in her bed and looked at the fire dancing on the ceiling, and all the time the island seemed to be coming closer and closer to the house. They were sleeping by a meadow near the shore, with patches of snow on the covers, and under them the ice darkened and began to glide. A channel opened very slowly in the floor, and all their luggage floated out in the river of moonlight. All the suitcases were open and full of darkness and moss, and none of them ever came back.

Sophia reached out her hand and pulled her grandmother's braid, very gently. Grandmother woke up instantly.

"Listen," Sophia whispered. "I saw two fires in the window. Why are there two fires instead of one?"

Her grandmother thought for a moment and said, "It's because we have double windows."

After a while Sophia asked, "Are you sure the door is closed?"

"It's open," her grandmother said. "It's always open; you can sleep quite easy."

Sophia rolled up in the quilt. She let the whole island float out on the ice and on to the horizon. Just before she fell asleep, her father got up and put more wood in the stove.

The Magic Forest

ON THE OUTSIDE of the island, beyond the bare
rock, there was a stand of dead forest. It lay right in
the path of the wind and for many hundreds of
years had tried to grow directly into the teeth of
every storm, and had thus acquired an appearance
all its own. From a passing rowboat it was obvious
that each tree was stretching away from the wind;
they crouched and twisted, and many of them crept.
Eventually the trunks broke or rotted and then
sank, the dead trees supporting or crushing those
still green at the top. All together they formed a
tangled mass of stubborn resignation. The ground
was shiny with brown needles, except where the
spruces had decided to crawl instead of stand, their
greenery luxuriating in a kind of frenzy, damp and
glossy as if in a jungle. This forest was called "the
magic forest." It had shaped itself with slow and
laborious care, and the balance between survival
and extinction was so delicate that even the smallest
change was unthinkable. To open a clearing or
separate the collapsing trunks might lead to the
ruin of the magic forest. The marshy spots could

not be drained, and nothing could be planted behind the dense, sheltering wall of trees. Deep under this thicket, in places where the sun never shone, there lived birds and small animals. In calm weather you could hear the rustle of wings and hastily scurrying feet, but the animals never showed themselves.

In the beginning, the family tried to make the magic forest more terrible than it was. They collected stumps and dry juniper bushes from neighboring islands and rowed them back to the forest. Huge specimens of weathered, whitened beauty were dragged across the island. They splintered and cracked and made broad, empty paths to the places where they were to stand. Grandmother could see that it wasn't turning out, but she said nothing. Afterward, she cleaned the boat and waited until the rest of the family tired of the magic forest. Then she went in by herself. She crawled slowly past the marsh and the ferns, and when she got tired she lay down on the ground and looked up through the network of gray lichens and branches. Later, the others asked her where she had been, and she replied that maybe she had slept a little while.

Except for the magic forest, the island became an orderly, beautiful park. They tidied it down to the smallest twig while the earth was still soaked with spring rain, and, after that, they stuck carefully to the narrow paths that wandered through the carpet of moss from one granite outcropping to another and down to the sand beach. Only farmers and summer guests walk on the moss. What they don't know—and it cannot be repeated too often— is that moss is terribly frail. Step on it once and it rises the next time it rains. The second time, it doesn't rise back up. And the third time you step on moss, it dies. Eider ducks are the same way—the third time you frighten them up from their nests, they never come back. Sometime in July the moss would adorn itself with a kind of long, light grass. Tiny clusters of flowers would open at exactly the same height above the ground and sway together in the wind, like inland meadows, and the whole island would be covered with a veil dipped in heat, hardly visible and gone in a week. Nothing could give a stronger impression of untouched wilderness.

But Grandmother sat in the magic forest and carved outlandish animals. She cut them from branches and driftwood and gave them paws and faces, but she only hinted at what they looked like and never made them too distinct. They retained their wooden souls, and the curve of their backs and legs had the enigmatic shape of growth itself and remained a part of the decaying forest. Sometimes she cut them directly out of a stump or the trunk of a tree. Her carvings became more and more numerous. They clung to trees or sat astride the branches, they rested against the trunks or settled into the ground. With outstretched arms, they sank in the marsh, or they curled up quietly and slept by a root. Sometimes they were only a profile in the shadows, and sometimes there were two or three together, entwined in battle or in love. Grandmother worked only in old wood that had already found its form. That is, she saw and selected those pieces of wood that expressed what she wanted them to say.

One time she found a big white vertebra in the sand. It was too hard to work but could not have been made any prettier anyway, so she put it in the magic forest as it was. She found more bones, white or gray, all washed ashore by the sea.

"What is it you're doing?" Sophia asked.

"I'm playing," Grandmother said.

Sophia crawled into the magic forest and saw everything her grandmother had done.

"Is it an exhibit?" she asked.

But Grandmother said it had nothing to do with sculpture, sculpture was another thing completely.

They started gathering bones together along the shore.

Gathering is peculiar, because you see nothing but what you're looking for. If you're picking raspberries, you see only what's red, and if you're looking for bones you see only the white. No matter where you go, the only thing you see is bones. Sometimes they are as thin as needles, extremely fine and delicate, and have to be handled with great care. Sometimes they are large, heavy thighbones, or a cage of ribs buried in the sand like the timbers of a shipwreck. Bones come in a thousand shapes and every one of them has its own structure.

Sophia and Grandmother carried everything they found to the magic forest. They would usually go at sundown. They decorated the ground under the trees with bone arabesques like ideographs, and when they finished their patterns they would sit for a while and talk, and listen to the movements of the birds in the thicket. Once, they flushed a grouse, and another time they saw a tiny owl. It was sitting on a branch, silhouetted against the evening sky. No one had ever seen an owl on the island before.

One morning Sophia found a perfect skull of some large animal—found it all by herself. Grandmother thought it was a seal skull. They hid it in a basket and waited all day until evening. The sunset was in different shades of red, and the light flooded in over the whole island so that even the ground turned scarlet. They put the skull in the magic forest, and it lay on the ground and gleamed with all its teeth.

Suddenly Sophia began to scream.

"Take it away!" she screamed. "Take it away!"

Grandmother picked her up and held her but thought it best not to say anything. After a while Sophia went to sleep. Grandmother sat and thought about building a matchbox house on the sandy beach by the blueberry patch behind the house. They could build a dock and make windows out of tinfoil.

And so the wooden animals were allowed to vanish into their forest. The arabesques sank into the ground and turned green with moss, and the trees slipped deeper and deeper into each other's arms as time went by. Grandmother often went to the magic forest when the sun went down. But in the daytime she sat on the veranda steps and made boats of bark.

The Scolder

ONE MORNING before dawn it got very cold in the guest room. Grandmother dragged the rag rug up on the bed and pulled some raincoats down from the wall, but they didn't help much. She supposed it was due to the bog. It's a funny thing about bogs. You can fill them with rocks and sand and old logs and make a little fenced-in yard on top with a woodpile and a chopping block—but bogs go right on behaving like bogs. Early in the spring they breathe ice and make their own mist, in remembrance of the time when they had black water and their own sedge blossoming untouched. Grandmother looked at the oil stove, which had gone out, and at the clock, which said three. Then she got out of bed and put on her clothes, took her walking stick, and hobbled down the stone steps. It was a dead-calm night, and she wanted to listen to the long-tailed ducks.

It was not only the woodyard: the whole island was covered with fog, and there was that special early May silence near the sea. The branches of the trees dripped water, clearly audible in the silence. Nothing was growing yet, and there were patches of snow in sheltered places, but the landscape was brimming with expectation. She heard the cry of the long-tailed ducks. They are called scolders, because their cry is a steady, chiding chatter, farther and farther away, farther and farther out. People rarely see them. They are as secretive as corncrakes. But a corncrake hides in a meadow all alone, while the long-tails are out beyond the farthest islands in enormous wedding flocks, singing all through the spring night.

Grandmother walked up over the bare granite and thought about birds in general. It seemed to her no other creature had the same dramatic capacity to underline and perfect events—the shifts in the seasons and the weather, the changes that run through people themselves. She thought about migratory birds, and the thrush on a summer evening, and the cuckoo—yes, the cuckoo—and the great, cold birds that sail and watch, and the very small birds that sweep in for hasty visits in large late-summer parties, chubby, dumb, and unafraid, and about the swallows that only honor houses where the people are happy. It seemed remarkable that the impersonal birds should have become such powerful symbols. Or maybe not. For Grandmother, long-tailed ducks meant anticipation and renewal. She walked carefully across the rock on her stiff legs, and when she came to the little cottage she knocked on the window. Sophia woke up at once and came outside.

"I'm going to go listen to the long-tails," Grandmother said.

Sophia got dressed and they walked on together. On the east side of the island, there were small borders of ice around the rocks. No one had had time to gather driftwood yet, and the whole shore was a tangle, a broad bulging mass of tumbled planks and seaweed and reeds along with posts and fragile wooden boxes that had turned inside out around their steel frames, and on top of everything lay an enormous, heavy log that was black with oil-

spill. Small pieces of bark and the splinters of old
storms rocked in the water beyond the rim of ice,
drawn slowly out and in again by a feeble swell. It
was very close to sunrise, and the fog out over the
sea was already suffused with light. The long-tailed
ducks kept up their steady call, distant and me-
lodious.

"They're breeding," Sophia said.

The sun came up. The fog glowed for an instant
and then simply vanished. Out on a flat rock in the
water lay a scolder. It was wet and dead and looked
like a wrung-out plastic bag. Sophia declared that it
was an old crow, but Grandmother didn't believe
her.

"But it's spring!" Sophia said. "They don't die
now; they're brand new and just married—that's
what you said!"

"Well," Grandmother said, "it did die now, all
the same."

"How did it die?" Sophia yelled. She was very
angry.

"Of unrequited love," her grandmother explained. "He sang and scolded all night for his
scolder hen and then along came another and stole
her away, so he put his head under the water and
floated away."

"That's not true," Sophia screamed. She started
to cry. "Long-tails can't drown. Tell it right!"

So Grandmother told her he had simply hit his head on a rock. He was singing and scolding so hard that he didn't look where he was going, and so it just happened, right when he was happier than he'd ever been before.

"That's better," Sophia said. "Shall we bury him?"

"It's not necessary," Grandmother said. "The tide will come in and he'll bury himself. Seabirds are supposed to be buried at sea, like sailors."

They walked on and talked about burial at sea, and the long-tails sang in dyads and triads, farther and farther away. The neck of land out toward the point was completely transformed by the winter storms. There had never been anything but rocks out there, but now the whole shore was sand.

"We ought to save it," Grandmother said, poking the sand with her stick. "If the sea rises and we get a north wind, all of it will wash back out again."

She stretched out full length on a bed of whitened reeds and looked at the sky. Sophia lay down beside her. It was growing warmer all the time, and after a while they heard the curiously chilly, somehow veiled sound of migratory birds in flight and watched a whole flock fly in over the island toward the northeast.

"What'll we do now?" Sophia said.

Grandmother suggested that Sophia walk around the point and see what had drifted ashore.

"Are you sure you won't be bored?" Sophia asked.

"Absolutely sure," Grandmother said.

She turned on her side and put her arm over her head. Between the arm of her sweater, her hat, and the white reeds, she could see a triangle of sky, sea, and sand—quite a small triangle. There was a blade of grass in the sand beside her, and between its sawtoothed leaves it held a piece of seabird down. She carefully observed the construction of this piece of down—the taut white rib in the middle, surrounded by the down itself, which was pale brown and lighter than the air, and then darker and shiny toward the tip, which ended in a tiny but spirited curve. The down moved in a draft of air too slight for her to feel. She noted that the blade of grass and the down were at precisely the right distance for her eyes. She wondered if the down had caught on the grass now, in the spring, maybe during the night, or if it had been there all winter. She saw the conical depression in the sand at the foot of the blade of grass and the wisp of seaweed that had twined around the stem. Right next to it lay a piece of bark. If you looked at it for a long time it grew and became a very ancient mountain. The upper side had craters and excavations that looked like whirlpools. The scrap of bark was beautiful and dramatic. It rested above its shadow on a single point of contact, and the grains of sand were coarse, clean, almost gray in the morning light, and the sky was completely clear, as was the sea.

Sophia came back, running.

"I found a floor grate!" she hollered. "It's big; it's from a ship! It's as long as a boat!"

"You don't say!" her grandmother said.

It was important for her not to stand up too quickly, so she had time to watch the blade of grass just as the down left its hold and was borne away in a light morning breeze. It was carried out of her field of vision, and when she got on her feet the landscape had grown smaller.

"I saw a feather," she said. "A piece of scolder down."

"What scolder?" Sophia said, for she had forgotten the bird that died of love.

Berenice

ONE SUMMER Sophia had a guest of her own—her first friend to come visit. It was a fairly new friend, a little girl whose hair she admired. Her name was

Herdice Evelyn, but everyone called her Pipsan.

Sophia explained to her grandmother that Pipsan was scared of being asked her real name, and
that actually she was scared of everything, so you
had to be very careful with her, and they decided
not to frighten Pipsan, at least in the beginning,
with things she had never seen before. When Pipsan arrived, she was dressed wrong and had shoes
with leather soles. She was too well bred and terribly quiet, and her hair was so beautiful it took
your breath away.

"Isn't it lovely?" Sophia whispered. "Naturally
curly."

"Very lovely," Grandmother said.

They looked at each other and nodded slowly,
and Sophia sighed.

"I've decided to be her protector," she said.
"Couldn't we have a secret society to be her pro-
tectors? The only sad thing is that 'Pipsan' doesn't
sound aristocratic."

Grandmother proposed that they call the child
Berenice, but only within the society of course.
Berenice was a queen, renowned for her hair, and
also a constellation.

Surrounded by this secret imagery, and the subject of much serious conversation, Pipsan wandered
about the island, an unusually small and timid child
who could not be left alone. As a result, Sophia was

always in a hurry. She didn't dare leave her guest
to herself for more than a few minutes at a time.

Grandmother lay in the guest room at the back
of the house and heard her coming. She puffed up
the stairs, burst into the room, and sat down on the
bed.

"She's driving me crazy," she whispered. "She
won't learn to row because she's scared to go out in
the boat. She says the water's too cold. What are
we going to do with Berenice?"

They held a short meeting on the subject, without deciding anything for the time being, and
Sophia rushed out again.

The guest room had been a later addition to
the house and therefore had a character of its own.
It clung tightly to the back of the original building,
and its inner wall was tarred. On this wall hung the
nets, along with ringbolts and rope and other items
that might come in handy and had always hung
there. The roof, which was a continuation of the
regular roof, was very steep, and the room rested
on posts, because the rock on which the house stood
dropped straight down into what had once been a
bog between the building and the woodyard. There
was a pine tree outside, which restricted the guest
room to an area not much longer than a bed. It was,
in effect, nothing but a short corridor, painted blue,
with the door and the nail kegs at one end and a

window that was much too large at the other. The window was large because it was left over, and it slanted on one side because of the roof. The bed was white, with ornamentation in blue and gold. Underneath the guest room, they stored lumber, empty cartons, picks and shovels, cans of coal tar, gasoline, and wood preservative, plus some ageing bait boxes and other odds and ends still too good to be thrown away. In other words, the guest room was a very pleasant place, quite distinct from the rest of the house. The details don't really matter.

Grandmother went back to her book and more or less forgot about Berenice. From the southwest came a steady summer wind that whispered sleepily around the house and on across the island. She could hear the weather report on the radio inside the house. A corner of sunshine edged across the windowsill.

Sophia banged open the door and came in.

"She's crying," she said. "She's afraid of ants, and she thinks they're all over the place. She just keeps lifting her feet, like this, and stamping, and crying. She's scared to stand still. What are we going to do with her?"

They decided to take Berenice out in the boat, where there weren't any ants, and thus coax her away from a greater fear into a lesser one, and Grandmother went back to her book.

By the foot of her bed there was a nice painting
of a hermit. It was a color reproduction on shiny
paper and had been cut out of a book. It showed a
desert in deep twilight, nothing but sky and dry
earth. In the middle was the hermit, lying in his
bed reading. He was in a kind of open tent, and beside him was a bedside table with an oil lamp. The
whole space occupied by the tent, the bed, the table,
and the circle of light was hardly larger than the
man himself. Farther off in the dusk were the vague
outlines of a lion at rest. Sophia found the lion
threatening, but Grandmother felt it was there to
protect the hermit.

When the southwest wind was blowing, the
days seemed to follow one another without any kind
of change or occurrence; day and night, there was
the same even, peaceful rush of wind. Papa worked
at his desk. The nets were set out and taken in.
They all moved about the island doing their own
chores, which were so natural and obvious that no
one mentioned them, neither for praise nor sym-
pathy. It was just the same long summer, always,
and everything lived and grew at its own pace. The
arrival on the island of the child Berenice—we shall
call her by her secret name—involved complications
that no one had foreseen. They had never realized
that their casual island household was in fact an
indivisible unit. Their absent-minded manner of

living in time with the leisurely course of the summer had never had a guest to reckon with, and they
could not see that the child Berenice was more
afraid of them than she was of the sea and the ants
and the wind in the trees at night.

On the third day, Sophia came into the guest
room and said, "Well, that does it. She's impossible.
I got her to dive, but it didn't help."

"Did she really dive?" Grandmother asked.

"Yes, really. I gave her a shove and she dived."

"Oh," Grandmother said. "And then what?"

"Her hair can't take salt water," explained
Sophia sadly. "It looks awful. And it was her hair
I liked."

Grandmother threw off the blanket and stood
up and took her walking stick. "Where is she?"
she asked.

"In the potato patch," Sophia said.

Grandmother walked across the island to the
potato patch. It lay a short way from the water, in
a lee among some rocks, and had the sun all day.
They always set out an early variety of seed potatoes on a bed of sand and then covered them with a
layer of seaweed. They watered them with salt
water, and the plants produced small, clean, oval
potatoes with a pinkish luster. The child was sitting
behind a large rock, half hidden beneath the
branches of a pine. Grandmother sat down nearby

and started digging with her trowel. The potatoes were still too small, but she dug up a dozen or so all the same.

"Here's what you do," she said to Berenice. "You plant a big one and it turns into a lot of little ones. And if you wait, they all get big."

Berenice looked at her from under a tangle of hair, quickly, and then looked away again. She didn't care about potatoes, or people, or anything at all.

If only she were a little bigger, Grandmother thought. Preferably a good deal bigger, so I could tell her that I understand how awful it is. Here you come, headlong, into a tight little group of people who have always lived together, who have the habit of moving around each other on land they know and own and understand, and every threat to what they're used to only makes them still more compact and self-assured. An island can be dreadful for someone from outside. Everything is complete, and everyone has his obstinate, sure, and self-sufficient place. Within their shores, everything functions according to rituals that are as hard as rock from repetition, and at the same time they amble through their days as whimsically and casually as if the world ended at the horizon. Grandmother thought about all these things so intensely that she forgot about the potatoes and Berenice. She gazed out over

the lee shore to the waves that swept around the island on both sides and then rejoined and moved on
toward the mainland—a long blue landscape of
vanishing waves that left only a small wedge of
quiet water behind them. A fishing boat with a big
white moustache was sailing across the bay.

"Oh look!" Grandmother said. "There goes a
boat."

She looked around for Berenice, but by this
time the child had concealed herself completely
beneath the tree.

"Oh look!" said Grandmother once again. "Here
come some bad men. We better hide."

With some difficulty, she crawled in under the
pine tree.

"See?" she whispered. "There they are. They're
coming. You better follow me to a safer place."

She started crawling across the rock and Berenice followed along on all fours at a furious pace.
They made their way around the little bilberry bog
and came to a hollow full of willow bushes. The
ground was wet, but that couldn't be helped.

"That was close," said Grandmother. "But
we're safe for the moment."

She looked at the expression on Berenice's face
and added, "I mean we're safe. They'll never find
us here."

"Why are they bad?" whispered Berenice.

"Because they're coming to bother us," Grandmother said. "We live here on this island, and people who come to bother us should stay away."

The fishing boat sailed on by. Sophia hunted for them. She looked for half an hour, and when she finally found them, quietly teasing some tadpoles, she was angry.

"Where have you been?" she screamed. "I've looked all over!"

"We hid," Grandmother explained.

"We hid," Berenice repeated. "We won't let anyone come bother us." She walked over very close to Grandmother and stared hard at Sophia.

Sophia didn't answer but turned abruptly and ran away.

The island shrank and grew crowded. Wherever she went, she was aware of where they were. She had to stay away from them, but the minute they disappeared she was forced to search them out so she could ignore them again.

After a while, Grandmother got tired and started up the guest room stairs.

"I'm going to read for a while," she said. "You go play with Sophia."

"No," said Berenice.

"Well, then, play by yourself."

"No," said Berenice. She was scared again.

Grandmother went after a pad of paper and a charcoal pencil and put them down on the steps.

"Draw a picture," she said.

"I don't know anything to draw," the child said.

"Draw something awful," Grandmother said, for she was really tired now. "Draw the awfullest thing you can think of, and take as much time as you possibly can."

Then she closed and latched the door and lay down on the bed and pulled the covers up over her head. The southwest wind whispered peacefully, distantly in from the sea and enveloped the island's inner core—the guest room and the woodyard.

Sophia pulled the bait box up to the window and climbed up and gave three long and three short knocks on the windowpane. When Grandmother emerged from her blankets and opened the window a crack, Sophia informed her that she had withdrawn from the society.

"That Pipsan!" she said. "I'm not interested in Pipsan. What's she doing?"

"She's drawing. She's drawing the awfullest thing she can think of."

"She can't draw," whispered Sophia passionately. "Did you give her my pad? What does she have to draw for?"

The window slammed shut, and Grandmother

lay down again. Sophia came back three times, each
time with a dreadful picture, which she pasted up
on the window facing in toward the guest room.
The first picture showed a child with ugly hair who
stood screaming as large ants crawled over her
body. The second showed the same child being hit
on the head with a stone. The third was a more general view of a shipwreck, from which Grandmother
concluded that Sophia had worked off her anger.
When she had opened her book and found her
place at last, a paper came sliding through the crack
under the door.

Berenice's drawing was good. It had been done
in a kind of painstaking fury, and depicted a creature with a black hole for a face. This creature was
moving forward with its shoulders hunched. Its
arms were long scalloped wings, like those on a
bat. They began near its neck and dragged on the
ground on either side, a prop or perhaps a hindrance
for the vague, boneless body. It was such an awful
and such an expressive picture that Grandmother
was filled with admiration. She opened the door and
called, "It's good! It's a really good drawing!" She
didn't look at the child, only at the drawing, and
the tone of her voice was neither friendly nor en-
couraging.

Berenice remained seated on the steps and did
not turn around. She picked up a little stone and

threw it straight up in the air, whereupon she stood up and walked slowly and dramatically down toward the water. Sophia stood on the woodpile and waited.

"What's she doing now?" Grandmother asked.

"She's throwing stones in the water," Sophia said. "She's going out on the point."

"That's good," Grandmother said. "Come here and look at what she did. What do you think?"

"Well, yes . . ." Sophia said.

Grandmother put the picture up on the wall with a couple of thumbtacks.

"It's very original," she said. "Now let's leave her in peace."

"*Can* she draw?" asked Sophia gloomily.

"No," Grandmother said. "Probably not. She's probably one of those people who do one good thing and then that's the end of it."

The Pasture

SOPHIA ASKED her grandmother what Heaven looked like, and Grandmother said it might be like the pasture they were just then walking by on their way to the village. They stopped to look. It was very hot, the road was white and cracked, and all the plants along the ditch had dust on their leaves. They walked into the pasture and sat down in the grass, which was tall and not a bit dusty. It was full of bluebells and cat's-foot and buttercups.

"Are there ants in Heaven?" Sophia asked.

"No," said Grandmother, and lay down carefully on her back. She propped her hat on her nose and tried to sneak a little sleep. Some kind of farm machinery was running steadily and peacefully in the distance. If you turned it off—which was easy to do—and listened only to the insects, you could hear thousands of millions of them, and they filled the whole world with rising and falling waves of ecstasy and summer. Sophia picked some flowers and held them in her hand until they got warm and unpleasant; then she put them down on her grandmother and asked how God could keep track of all the people who prayed at the same time.

"He's very, very smart," Grandmother mumbled sleepily under her hat.

"Answer really," Sophia said. "How does He have time?"

"He has secretaries . . ."

"But how does He manage to do what you pray for if He doesn't get time to talk to the secretary before it's too late?"

Grandmother pretended to be asleep, but she

knew she wasn't fooling anyone, and so finally she
said that He'd made it so nothing bad could happen between the moment you prayed and the moment He found out what you prayed for. And then
Sophia wanted to know what happened if you
prayed while you were falling out of a tree and you
were halfway down.

"Aha," said Grandmother, perking up. "In that
case He makes you catch on a limb."

"That is smart," Sophia admitted. "Now you get
to ask. But it has to be about Heaven."

"Do you think all the angels wear dresses, so
no one can tell what kind they are?"

"What a dumb question! You know they all
wear dresses. But now listen carefully: if one of
them wants to know for sure what kind another
one is, he just flies under him and looks to see if
he's wearing pants."

"I see," Grandmother said. "That's good to
know. Now it's your turn."

"Can angels fly down to Hell?"

"Of course. They might have all sorts of friends
and neighbors down there."

"Now I've got you!" Sophia cried. "Yesterday
you said there wasn't any Hell!"

Grandmother was annoyed and sat up angrily.

"And I say exactly the same thing today," she
said. "But this is just a game."

"It's not a game! It's serious when you're talking about God!"

"He would never do anything so dumb as make a Hell."

"Of course He did."

"No He didn't!"

"Yes He did! A big enormous Hell!"

Because she was mad, Grandmother stood up much too quickly, and the whole pasture started spinning around and she almost lost her balance. She waited for the giddiness to stop.

"Sophia," she said, "this is really not something to argue about. You can see for yourself that life is hard enough without being punished for it afterwards. We get comfort when we die, that's the whole idea."

"It's not hard at all!" Sophia shouted. "And what are you going to do about the Devil, then? He *lives* in Hell!"

For a moment Grandmother considered saying that there was no Devil either, but she didn't want to be mean. The farm machinery was making a terrible racket. She walked back toward the road and stepped right in a cow pie. Her grandchild was not behind her.

"Sophia," called Grandmother warningly. "I said you could have an orange when we got to the store . . ."

"An orange!" said Sophia contemptuously. "Do you think people care about oranges when they're talking about God and the Devil?"

Grandmother poked the cow dung off her shoe with her walking stick as well as she could.

"My dear child," she said, "with the best will in the world I cannot start believing in the Devil at my age. You can believe what you like, but you must learn to be tolerant."

"What does that mean?" asked the child sullenly.

"That means respecting other people's convictions."

"What are convictions?" Sophia screamed and stamped her foot.

"Letting others believe what they want to believe!" her grandmother shouted back. "I'll let you believe God damns people and you let me not."

"You swore," Sophia whispered.

"I certainly did not."

"You did too. You said 'God damns.' "

They were no longer looking at each other. Three cows came down the road, switching their tails and swaying their heads. They passed slowly by in a swarm of flies and walked on toward the village, with the skin on their rear ends puckering and twitching as they went. Then they were gone, leaving nothing but silence.

Finally Sophia's grandmother said, "I know a song you don't know." She waited for a minute, and then she sang—way off key because her vocal cords were crooked:

> Cow pies are free,
> Tra-la-la
> But don't throw them at me.
> Tra-la-la
> For you too could get hit
> Tra-la-la
> With cow shit!

"*What* did you *say?*" Sophia whispered, because she couldn't believe her ears. And Grandmother sang the same really awful song again.

Sophia climbed over the ditch and started toward the village.

"Papa would never say 'shit,'" she said over her shoulder. "Where did you learn that song?"

"I'm not telling," Grandmother said.

They came to the barn and climbed the stile and walked through the Nybonda's barnyard, and before they got to the store under the trees, Sophia had learned the song and could sing it just as badly as her grandmother did.

Playing Venice

ONE SATURDAY there was mail for Sophia—a picture postcard from Venice. Her whole name was on the address side, with "Miss" in front, and on the shiny side was the prettiest picture anyone in the family had ever seen. There was a long row of pink and gilded palaces rising from a dark waterway that mirrored the lanterns on several slim gondolas. The full moon was shining in a dark blue sky, and a beautiful, lonely woman stood on a little bridge with one hand covering her eyes. The picture was tinged with real gold here and there in appropriate places. They put the postcard up on the wall under the barometer.

Sophia wanted to know why all the buildings were standing in the water, and her grandmother told her all about Venice and how it is sinking into the sea. She had been there herself once. The memory of her trip to Italy exhilarated her, and she talked on and on. Occasionally she tried to tell about other places she had seen, but Sophia wanted only to hear about Venice, and especially about the dark canals that smelled of must and rot and that each year pulled the city farther down into the mud, down into a soft black slime where golden dinner plates lay buried. There is something very elegant about throwing the plates out the window after dinner, and about living in a house that is slowly sinking to its doom. "Look, Mama," said the lovely Venetian girl, "the kitchen is under water today." "Dear child, it doesn't matter," her mother replied. "We still have the drawing room." They rode down in their elevator and stepped into a gondola and glided through the streets. There wasn't an automobile in the entire city, they had all long since sunk into the ooze. The only sound was footsteps on the bridges, and people walked and walked all night. Sometimes one heard a strain of music, and sometimes a creaking noise as some palace settled and sank deeper. And the smell of mud was everywhere.

Sophia went down to the marsh pool, which was a smooth brownish-black under the alder trees. She dug a canal through the moss and the bilberry bushes. "Mama, my ring has fallen in the canal." Her ring was gold, with a red ruby. "Dear child, don't trouble yourself. We have the whole drawing room full of gold and precious jewels."

Sophia went to her grandmother and said, "Call me 'Dear Child' and I'll call you 'Mama.' "

"But I'm your grandmother," Grandmother said.

"Please, Mama, it's a game," Sophia explained. "Mama, shall we play you're my grandmother? I am your dear child from Venice, and I've made a canal."

Grandmother stood up. "I know a better game," she said. "We'll be old Venetians building a new Venice."

They started building in the marsh pool. They made pilings for the Piazza San Marco out of a lot of little wooden plugs, and covered them with flat stones. They dug additional canals and built bridges over them. Black ants scurried back and forth across the bridges, while down below there were gondolas gliding along in the moonlight. Sophia collected pieces of white marble along the shore.

"Look, Mama," she called. "I've found a new palace."

"But my dear child, I'm only 'Mama' to your father," Grandmother said. She was concerned.

"Is that so!" Sophia shouted. "Why is he the only one who gets to say 'Mama'?"

She threw the palace in the water and stalked away.

Grandmother sat down on the veranda to make a Doge's Palace out of balsa wood. When the palace was done, she painted it with watercolors and gold. Sophia came to look at it.

"In this palace," Grandmother said, "there lives

a mother and a father and their daughter. Right through that window. The daughter has just thrown the dinner plates out the window, and they broke on the piazza, because they were only china. I wonder what the mother said."

"I know what the mother said," Sophia declared. "She said, 'My dear child, do you think there's no end to your mother's china?' "

"And what did the daughter say?"

"She said, 'Forgive me, Mama. I promise to throw only the golden dinner plates in the future!' "

They set the palace by the piazza, and the father, mother, and daughter continued to live there. Grandmother made more palaces. A great many families moved into Venice and called to one another across the canals. "How far did your palace sink today?" "Oh, it's not so bad. Mother says it's only a foot or so." "What's your mother making for dinner? My mother's boiling some perch." At night they all slept soundly, and the only noise was the footsteps of the ants across the bridges.

Grandmother became more and more involved. She made a hotel and a trattoria and a campanile with a little lion on top. It was a very long time since she'd been in Venice and she could remember the names of all the streets, because her memory was best for things that had happened long ago.

One day, there was a green salamander in the Grand Canal and traffic had to make a long detour.

That same evening, it started to rain, and the wind went over to the southeast. The radio said low-pressure system and winds to thirty miles an hour, but no one gave it a second thought. But when Grandmother woke up in the middle of the night as usual, and heard rain pelting on the roof, she remembered the sinking city, and it worried her. It was blowing hard, and there was nothing but a grassy beach between the marsh and the sea. Grandmother dozed off and woke up again several times, and each time she heard the rain and the waves and worried about Venice and Sophia. When it started to get light, she got up and put on a slicker over her nightgown and covered her head with a sou'wester.

The rain had let up, but the ground was drenched and dark. It will make everything grow, she thought absent-mindedly. She took a firm grip on her walking stick and stumbled on against the wind. It was a beautiful gray dawn, with long parallel rainclouds marching across the sky and whitecaps covering the dark green sea. She could see right away that the whole shore line was flooded, and then she saw Sophia running toward her across the rock.

"It's sunk," Sophia screamed. "She's gone!"

The cottage was open, and the door stood banging in the wind.

"Go back to bed," Grandmother said. "Take off your nightgown, it's wet through, and close the door and go to bed. I'll find the palace. I promise I'll find it."

Sophia was crying with her mouth wide open. She wasn't listening. Finally Grandmother had to go with her to the cottage to be sure she went back to bed.

"I'll find the palace," she told her again. "Now stop howling and go to sleep."

She closed the door and walked back down toward the shore. When she got there, she found that the marsh had become a bay. The waves washed up into the heather and swept back into the sea again, and the alders stood well out in the water. Venice had disappeared beneath the sea.

Grandmother stood gazing at this scene for quite a while; then she turned and went home. She lit the lamp and got out her tools and a suitable piece of balsa wood and put on her glasses.

The Doge's Palace was ready at seven o'clock, just as Sophia banged on the door.

"Wait a minute," Grandmother said. "It's latched."

"Did you find her?" Sophia called. "Was she still there?"

"Yes, of course," Grandmother answered. "They were all still there."

The palace looked much too new, not as if it had been through a flood. Quickly Grandmother took her water glass and poured it over the Doge's Palace, then emptied the ashtray into her hand and rubbed the cupolas and walls with ashes, and all the time Sophia kept pulling at the handle and yelling that she wanted in.

Grandmother opened the door. "We were lucky," she said.

Sophia examined the palace very carefully. She put it down on the night stand and didn't say a word.

"It's all right, isn't it?" said Grandmother anxiously.

"Quiet," Sophia whispered. "I want to hear if she's still there."

They listened for a long time. Then Sophia said, "You can rest easy. Her mother says it was a perfectly dreadful storm. Now she's cleaning up the mess, and she's pretty worn out."

"Yes, I'll bet she is," Grandmother said.

Dead Calm

THE SEA is very rarely so calm that a small boat with an outboard motor will venture out to The Cairn. The Cairn is the last island out in the Gulf of Finland. It takes hours to get there, and you have to take food for the entire day. The Cairn is a long skerry, and from a distance it looks like two islands, two smooth spines with a channel marker on one of them and a little beacon on the other. There is no cairn on the island at all. When you get closer, you can see that the granite spines are as sleek as seals and that there is a long thin neck of boulders between them. The boulders are perfectly round.

The sea was as smooth as oil, and so pale you could hardly tell it was blue. Grandmother sat in the middle of the boat under a violet parasol. She hated violet, but it was all they had. Moreover, it was really a pretty color, as clear and bright as the sea itself. The parasol made them look like the worst kind of summer people, which they were not. When they reached The Cairn, they went ashore at the first spot they came to, since there was no

lee side—in the calm all sides were lee. They carried
their things ashore and put the butter in the shade.
The granite was hot underfoot. Papa wedged the
handle of the parasol into a crack—Grandmother
was to lie there on an air mattress and enjoy herself.
She watched them set off in opposite directions; the
island was so large that pretty soon they turned into
little dots moving along the edge of the water. Then
she crawled out from under the parasol and took her
walking stick and headed off in a third direction of
her own, but before she left she arranged some
sweaters and bathrobes on the mattress so it would
look as though she were asleep.

Grandmother came down to the shore at an interesting spot where a little canyon cut through the
rock and ran out into the sea. Even now, at midday,
the bottom of this canyon was in shadow—right
down into the water and a long way out, like a
crevice of darkness. Grandmother sat down and
edged into the canyon a little at a time until at last
she dropped to the bottom and was all by herself in
peace and quiet. She lit a cigarette and watched the
barely visible swell. By and by, the boat appeared
from behind the point. Papa was making a sweep
around the reef to set out his nets.

"So there you are," Sophia said. "I went swimming."

"How's the water?" Grandmother said. From

the bottom of the canyon, the child was a narrow shadow against the sun, like a stick of wood.

"Pretty bloody cold," Sophia said, and jumped down into the canyon. The floor of the crevice was covered with stones, from the size of a person's head down to the size of a marble. They found a place where the granite was full of those very small Finnish garnets you find sometimes, and they tried to dig them out with a jackknife. It didn't work. It never does. They ate hard bread and watched the boat. All the nets were out, and it sailed back and disappeared around the point.

"You know, sometimes when everything's fine, I think it's just a bloody bore," Sophia said.

"You do?" said Grandmother, taking out another cigarette. It was only her second before noon, and she always tried to smoke in secret when she could remember to.

"Nothing *happens*," her grandchild explained. "I wanted to climb the channel marker and Papa said I couldn't."

"That's too bad," Grandmother said.

"No, it's not 'too bad,' " Sophia said. "It's bloody stupid."

"Where did you pick that up? You keep saying 'bloody' all the time."

"I don't know. It sounds neat."

"Violet's a bloody color," Grandmother said.

"Talk about 'bloody'—did I ever tell you about the dead pig I found once? We boiled the meat off for a week and it stunk to heaven. Your father wanted to have the skeleton for school. You know, for zoology."

"No," said Sophia suspiciously. "What do you mean? What school?"

"When your father was little."

"When? What pig? What did you say it was called?"

"Oh, nothing," Grandmother said. "One time when your father was little, about your age."

"He's big," the child said, and started cleaning the sand out from between her toes. They each fell silent. After a while, Grandmother said, "Right now he thinks I'm asleep under that umbrella."

"But you're not," Sophia said. "You're down here sneaking a cigarette."

They picked out stones that hadn't been worn completely round and threw them out into the water to make them rounder. The sun moved on across the sky, and the boat came around the point and took up the nets and dropped them right back in again.

"The fishing's bloody awful," Grandmother said.

"Listen," Sophia said. "I don't have time to stay here with you—I've only been in swimming twice today. You won't be sad now, will you?"

"I want to go too," Grandmother said.

Sophia thought for a moment and said, "All right; you can come too. But only where I tell you."

They helped each other climb out of the canyon, and then they circled around the hill so as not to be seen. Off to one side of the channel marker, there was a large, deep pool.

"Is this all right?" Sophia asked.

"It's fine," Grandmother said. She bared her legs and stuck them into the pool. The water was warm and pleasant. Some light brown muck swirled up to the surface, along with a swarm of tadpoles, but they quickly settled down again. She spread her toes and stuck her legs farther in. There was a big clump of loosestrife where the pool narrowed toward one end, and the granite was streaked with yellow sedum growing in the crevices. Papa had built a fire at the other end of the island, and the smoke rose straight up in the air.

"In all the years I've sailed around in these islands," Grandmother said, "I don't think it's ever been this calm before. There was always *some* wind. He never went out unless there was a storm. We had a spritsail. He'd sail the boat and I'd keep watch for the spar markers in the dark. I hardly had time—'north spar,' I'd say, and then 'west spar' —they went by so fast. And one time when the rudder came loose . . ."

"You fixed it with a hairpin," Sophia said.

Grandmother swished her legs in the pool and didn't say anything.

"Or maybe it was a safety pin," Sophia went on. "Some days I can't remember exactly. But who was *he?*"

"Your grandfather, of course," Grandmother said. "My husband."

"Are you married?" Sophia cried in great astonishment.

"Bloody nitwit," Grandmother muttered to herself. Out loud she said, "You better ask your father about generations and all that. Ask him to draw it on a piece of paper. If you're interested."

"I don't think so," said Sophia amiably. "I'm kind of busy right now."

The channel marker was a high wall of well-spaced, horizontal planks, like a section of picket fence turned on end. It was painted white, with a red triangle in the middle. The distance from one plank to the next was so great that Sophia's legs just barely reached, and after each step her knees began to shake—not much, just enough so that she had to wait until they stopped. Then came the next rung. Sophia had made it almost to the top before Grandmother saw her. Grandmother realized right away that she mustn't scream. She would have to wait for the child to come back down. It wasn't dangerous. Children have a lot of ape in them: they're good climbers and never fall unless they're startled.

Sophia was climbing very slowly now, with long pauses between steps, and Grandmother could see she was scared. The old woman stood up too quickly. Her walking stick rolled down into the pool, and the whole rock became an uncertain, hostile surface, arching and twisting in front of her. Sophia took one more step.

"You're doing fine," Grandmother called. "You're almost there!"

Sophia took another step. She got her hands over the topmost plank and didn't move.

"Now come back down," Grandmother said.

But the child didn't move. It was so hot in the sun that the channel marker shimmered and quaked in waves.

"Sophia!" Grandmother called. "My stick fell down in the pool and I can't walk." She waited and then called again. "It's bloody awful, do you hear me? My balance is bloody awful today, and I've got to have my cane!"

Sophia started down. She moved steadily, one step at a time.

Damned child, Grandmother thought. Confounded children. But that's what happens when people won't let you do anything fun. The people who are old enough.

Sophia was back down on the rock. She waded out into the pool for the stick and handed it to Grandmother without looking at her.

"You're a very good climber," said Grandmother sternly. "And brave, too, because I could see you were scared. Shall I tell him about it? Or shouldn't I?"

Sophia shrugged one shoulder and looked at her grandmother. "I guess maybe not," she said. "But you can tell it on your deathbed so it doesn't go to waste."

"That's a bloody good idea," Grandmother said. She walked off across the rock and sat down beside the air mattress, just outside the shade of the violet parasol.

The Cat

IT WAS a tiny kitten when it came and could drink its milk only from a nipple. Fortunately, they still had Sophia's baby bottle in the attic. In the beginning, the kitten slept in a tea cozy to keep warm, but when it found its legs they let it sleep in the cottage in Sophia's bed. It had its own pillow, next to hers.

It was a gray fisherman's cat and it grew fast. One day, it left the cottage and moved into the house, where it spent its nights under the bed in the box where they kept the dirty dishes. It had odd ideas of its own even then. Sophia carried the cat back to the cottage and tried as hard as she could to ingratiate herself, but the more love she gave it, the quicker it fled back to the dish box. When the box got too full, the cat would howl and someone would have to wash the dishes. Its name was Ma Petite, but they called it Moppy.

"It's funny about love," Sophia said. "The more you love someone, the less he likes you back."

"That's very true," Grandmother observed. "And so what do you do?"

"You go on loving," said Sophia threateningly. "You love harder and harder."

Her grandmother sighed and said nothing.

Moppy was carried around to all the pleasant places a cat might like, and he only glanced at them and walked away. He was flattened with hugs, endured them politely, and climbed back into the dish box. He was entrusted with burning secrets and merely averted his yellow gaze. Nothing in the world seemed to interest this cat but food and sleep.

"You know," Sophia said, "sometimes I think I

hate Moppy. I don't have the strength to go on loving him, but I think about him all the time!"

Week after week, Sophia pursued the cat. She
spoke softly and gave him comfort and understand-
ing, and only a couple of times did she lose her
patience and yell at him, or pull his tail. At such
times Moppy would hiss and run under the house,
and afterward his appetite was better and he slept
even longer than usual, curled up in unapproach-
able softness with one paw daintily across his nose.

Sophia stopped playing and started having
nightmares. She couldn't think about anything but
this cat who refused to be affectionate. Meanwhile,
Moppy grew into a lean and wild little animal, and
one June night he didn't come back to his dish box.
In the morning, he walked into the house and
stretched—front legs first, with his rear end up in
the air—then he closed his eyes and sharpened his
claws on the rocking chair, after which he jumped
up on the bed and went to sleep. The cat's whole
being radiated calm superiority.

He's started hunting, Grandmother thought.

She was right. The very next morning, the cat
came in and placed a small grayish-yellow bird on
the doorsill. Its neck had been deftly broken with
one bite, and some bright red drops of blood lay
prettily on the shiny coat of feathers. Sophia turned

pale and stared fixedly at the murdered bird. She sidled past Moppy, the murderer, with small, forced steps, and then turned and rushed out.

Later, Grandmother remarked on the curious fact that wild animals, cats for example, cannot understand the difference between a rat and a bird.

"Then they're dumb!" said Sophia curtly. "Rats are hideous, and birds are nice. I don't think I'll talk to Moppy for three days." And she stopped talking to her cat.

Every night, the cat went into the woods, and every morning it killed its prey and carried it into the house to be admired, and every morning the bird was thrown into the sea. A little while later, Sophia would appear outside the window and shout, "Can I come in? Have you taken out the body?" She punished Moppy and increased her own pain by means of a terrible coarseness. "Have you cleaned up the blood?" she would yell, or, "How many murdered today?" And morning coffee was no longer what it had been.

It was a great relief when Moppy finally learned to conceal his crimes. It is one thing to see a pool of blood and quite another thing only to know about it. Moppy probably grew tired of all the screaming and fussing, and perhaps he thought the family ate his birds. One morning when Grandmother was taking her first cigarette on the veranda, she dropped her holder and it rolled through a crack in the floor. She managed to raise one of the planks, and there was Moppy's handiwork—a row of small bird skeletons, all picked clean. Of course she knew that the cat had continued to hunt, and could not have stopped, but the next time he rubbed against her leg as he passed, she drew away and whispered, "You sly bastard." The cat dish stood, untouched, by the steps and attracted flies.

"You know what?" Sophia said. "I wish Moppy had never been born. Or else that I'd never been born. That would have been better."

"So you're still not speaking to each other?" Grandmother asked.

"Not a word," Sophia said. "I don't know what to do. And if I do forgive him—what fun is that when he doesn't even care?" Grandmother couldn't think of anything to say.

Moppy turned wild and rarely came into the house. He was the same color as the island—a light yellowish-gray with striped shadings like granite, or like sunlight on a sand bottom. When he slipped across the meadow by the beach, his progress was like a stroke of wind through the grass. He would watch for hours in the thicket, a motionless silhouette, two pointed ears against the sunset, and then suddenly vanish . . . and some bird would chirp, just once. He would slink under the creeping pines, soaked by the rain and lean as a streak, and he would wash himself voluptuously when the sun came out. He was an absolutely happy cat, but he didn't share with anyone. On hot days, he would roll on the smooth rock, and sometimes he would eat grass and calmly vomit his own hair the way cats do. And what he did between times no one knew.

One Saturday, the Övergårds came for coffee. Sophia went down to look at their boat. It was big, full of bags and jerry cans and baskets, and in one of the baskets a cat was meowing. Sophia lifted the lid and the cat licked her hand. It was a big, white cat with a broad face. It kept right on purring when she picked it up and carried it ashore.

"So you found the cat," said Anna Övergård. "It's a nice cat, but it's not a mouser, so we thought we'd give it to some friends."

Sophia sat on the bed with the heavy cat on her lap. It never stopped purring. It was soft and warm and submissive.

They struck a bargain easily, with a bottle of rum to close the deal. Moppy was captured and never knew what was happening until the Övergård's boat was on its way to town.

The new cat's name was Fluff. It ate fish and liked to be petted. It moved into Sophia's cottage and slept every night in her arms, and every morning it came in to morning coffee and slept some more in the bed beside the stove. If the sun was shining, it would roll on the warm granite.

"Not there!" Sophia yelled. "That's Moppy's place!" She carried the cat a little farther off, and it licked her on the nose and rolled obediently in the new spot.

The summer grew prettier and prettier, a long series of calm blue summer days. Every night, Fluff slept against Sophia's cheek.

"It's funny about me," Sophia said. "I think nice weather gets to be boring."

"Do you?" her grandmother said. "Then you're just like your grandfather, he liked storms too." But before she could say anything else about Grandfather, Sophia was gone.

And gradually the wind came up, sometime during the night, and by morning there was a regular southwester spitting foam all over the rocks.

"Wake up," Sophia whispered. "Wake up, kitty, precious, there's a storm."

Fluff purred and stretched warm sleepy legs in all directions. The sheet was covered with cat hair.

"Get up!" Sophia shouted. "It's a storm!" But the cat just turned over on its broad stomach. And suddenly Sophia was furious. She kicked open the door and threw the cat out in the wind and watched how it laid its ears back, and she screamed, "Hunt! Do something! Be like a cat!" And then she started to cry and ran to the guest room and banged on the door.

"What's wrong now?" Grandmother said.

"I want Moppy back!" Sophia screamed.

"But you know how it'll be," Grandmother said.

"It'll be awful," said Sophia gravely. "But it's Moppy I love."

And so they traded cats again.

The Cave

THERE WAS a deep bay on the largest of the nearby islands, and at the far end of this bay, the grass grew right in the sand, short and very green. Grass roots are extremely strong, they twist and tie themselves into a knotted mass that can stand up to the heaviest seas. Great ocean waves roll straight in over the sandy bottom, but once inside the bay, they meet the grass and flatten out. They dig away at the sand—they can do that much—but all that happens to the grass is that it sinks or rises, adjusting to new hills and gullies. A person could walk way out in the water and still feel the grass underfoot. Up toward shore, it grew out of the seaweed, and still farther up it made a jungle with the spiraea and the nettles and the vetch and all the other plants that like salt. This jungle was very thick and tall and lived mostly on dead seaweed and rotten fish. It grew as high as possible, and where it stopped it was met by sallow, rowan, and alder branches that bent down as far as they could reach. Walking between them with your arms outstretched was like swimming. Bird-cherry and rowan, especially rowan, smell like cat piss when they're in bloom.

Sophia made a path through this jungle with a pair of shears. She worked at it patiently whenever she was in the mood, and no one else knew about it. First, the path circled the rosebush, which was large and famous and had a name, Rosa Rugosa. When it blossomed, with its huge, wild roses that could take a storm and fell only when they wanted to, people came from the village to look. Its roots were high, washed clean by the waves, and there was seaweed in its branches. Every seven years, Rosa Rugosa died from salt and exposure, but then her children sprang up in the sand all around, so nothing changed. She had only moved a little. The path led on through a nasty patch of nettles, through the spiraea and the currant bushes and the loosestrife under the alder trees, and up to the big bird-cherry at the edge of the woods. On the right day, and with the right wind, you could lie down under a bird-cherry and all the petals would fall at the same time, but you had to watch out for aphids. They held onto the tree if left alone, but if you shook the branches the least little bit they fell right off.

After the bird-cherry, there are pine trees and moss, and the hill rises up from the beach, and every time, the cave is just as much of a surprise. It is so sudden. The cave is narrow and smells of rot, the walls are black and damp, and at the far end, there is a natural altar covered with green moss as fine and dense as plush.

"I know something you don't know," Sophia said. Grandmother put down her murder mystery and waited.

"Do you know what it is?" asked Sophia sternly.

"No," Grandmother said.

They rowed over to the island in the dory and tied up to a rock. Then they crept around the rose-bush. It was a good day for the secret path, because Grandmother was feeling dizzy and would really rather crawl than walk.

"These are nettles," she said.

"I told you that," Sophia said. "Crawl faster, it's only a little ways." They came to the spiraea and the loosestrife and the bird-cherry, and then Sophia turned around and said, "Now you can rest a while and smoke a cigarette." But Grandmother had left her matches at home. They lay down under the bird-cherry and thought, and Sophia asked what went on an altar.

"Something elegant and unusual," Grandmother said.

"Like what?"

"Oh, all sorts of things . . ."

"Say really!"

"I don't know right now," Grandmother said. She wasn't feeling well.

"Maybe a bunch of gold," Sophia suggested. "Though that's not specially unusual."

They crawled on through the pines, and Grandmother threw up in the moss.

"It could happen to anyone," the child said. "Did you take your Lupatro?"

Her grandmother stretched out on the ground and didn't answer.

After a while Sophia whispered, "I guess I can spare some time for you today."

It was nice and cool under the pine trees and they weren't in any hurry, so they slept for a while. When they woke up they crawled on to the cave, but Grandmother was too big to get in. "You'll have to tell me what it's like," she said.

"It's all green," Sophia said. "And it smells like rot and it's very pretty, and way at the back it's holy because that's where God lives, in a little box maybe."

"Is that so?" said Grandmother and stuck her head in as far as it would go. "And what are those?"

"Some old toadstools," Sophia said.

But Grandmother could see they were good mushrooms, and she took off her hat and sent her grandchild in to pick them, and they filled it up.

"Did you say He lived in a little box?" she said, and she took out the little sacred box, Lupatro, because it was empty now, and Sophia crawled back into the cave and put it on the altar.

They followed the path back around Rosa Rugosa and dug up one of her children to plant by the guest room steps. The roots came out easily for once, along with a lot of soil, and they packed the whole thing in a Gordon's Gin crate that was sticking up out of the seaweed. A little farther on, they found an old Russian cap for the mushrooms, so Grandmother could have her hat back.

"Just look how everything works out," Sophia said. "Is there anything else we need? Just say whatever you want!"

Grandmother said she was thirsty.

"Good," Sophia said. "You wait right here." She walked down the beach until she found a bottle in the sand, under water. It didn't have any label. They opened it and it fizzed. But it wasn't Vichy water, it was lemonade, which Grandmother much preferred.

"There, you see?" Sophia cried. "Everything works out! Now I'm going to find you a new watering can."

But Grandmother said she liked the old one fine. Moreover, she had a feeling that they shouldn't press their luck. They rowed home stern first. That sort of rowing is peaceful and pleasant, and it doesn't upset the stomach. It was after four o'clock when they got home, and the mushrooms were enough for the whole family.

The Road

IT WAS A BULLDOZER: an enormous, infernal, bright yellow machine that thundered and roared and floundered through the woods with clanging jaws. The men from the village scrambled on and around it like hysterical ants, trying to keep it headed in the right direction. "Jesus Christ!" Sophia shrieked without hearing what she said. She ran behind a rock with the milk can in one hand and watched the machine pluck up huge boulders that had lain in their moss for a thousand years, but now they just rose in the air and were tossed to one side, and there was a terrible cracking and splintering as pine trees gave way and were ripped from the ground with torn and broken roots. "Jesus, help! There go the woods!"

Sophia was trampling down the moss and shaking from head to foot in dread and rapture. There went a bird-cherry tree without a sound. It sank like a sigh, and up came shiny black earth, and the bulldozer took a new hold and bellowed on. The men shouted to each other nervously, which was no wonder since they were renting the machine, and it would cost them over a hundred marks an hour, including the trip from town and back. The machine was headed for the water, that was clear. It paid no attention to the path but pushed right on as straight as a herd of lemmings, for it was building a road to the sea.

It wouldn't be any fun to be an ant now, Sophia thought. A machine can do anything it wants! She went and collected the milk and the mail and walked back again, not on the path but on the broad, unprecedented road, which was suddenly very quiet. It was bordered on both sides by a sprawling chaos, as if huge hands had pressed back the forest, bent it and folded it like some soft grass that would never rise up again. The splintered white trunks of the trees were running with pitch, and farther from the road there was an immovable green mass; not a single branch and not one leaf was free to move in the wind. It was like walking between stone walls. The stones were drying and the soil that clung to them was turning gray. There were large gray patches on the new road, too. Severed roots stuck up everywhere. In places they formed a thin lacework filled with tiny clumps of earth that trembled on invisible wires as they dried in the sun. It was an altered landscape—breathless, like the silence after an explosion or a scream—and Sophia studied everything as she walked on down the new road, which seemed much longer than the old. The woods were silent. When she got down to the bay, she saw the bulldozer outlined against the water in all of its shapeless bulk. It had pushed its way down to the meadow by the beach and had then slid sideways into a hollow and kicked up a lot of sand. The grassy bank had given way, softly and treacherously, quite inexplicably, and the forest-eating monster lay there in silence at an unnatural angle, a picture of thwarted force. Beside the machine sat Emil Ehrström, smoking a cigarette.

"Where did everyone go?" Sophia asked.

"They went back to get some equipment," Emil said.

"What equipment?" Sophia said. And Emil said, "As if you knew anything about machines." Sophia walked on across the meadow, through the strong green mat of grass that storms can't kill—it only settles a bit and goes right on weaving its tight little roots. Grandmother was waiting by the boat out on the point. What a machine! Sophia thought. She'll be so surprised. It's like when God smote Gomorrah. It'll be a lot of fun to ride instead of walk.

Midsummer

THE FAMILY had one friend who never came too close, and that was Eriksson. He would drive by in his boat, or he would think about coming but never get around to it. There were even summers when Eriksson came nowhere near the island and didn't think about it, either.

Eriksson was small and strong and the color of the landscape, except that his eyes were blue. When people talked about him or thought about him, it seemed natural to lift their heads and gaze out over the sea. He was often unlucky and was plagued by bad weather and engine trouble. His herring nets would rip or get caught in his propeller, and fish and fowl would fail to turn up where he had expected them. And if he did have a good catch, the price would go down, so it was always

six of one or half a dozen of the other. But beyond
all these routine troubles that can spoil a person's
livelihood, there were other, unexpected possibili-
ties.

The family had long realized, without ever dis-
cussing it, that Eriksson didn't especially like fishing and hunting and motorboats. What he did like
was harder to put your finger on, but perfectly
understandable. His attention and his sudden
wishes raced here and there across the water like
ocean breezes, and he lived in a perpetual state of
quiet excitement. The sea is always subject to unusual events; things drift in or run aground or shift
in the night when the wind changes, and keeping
track of all this takes experience, imagination, and
unflagging watchfulness. It takes a good *nose*, to
put it simply. The big events always take place far
out in the skerries, and time is often of the essence.
Only small things happen in among the islands, but
these, too—the odd jobs that arise from the whims
of the summer people—have to be dealt with. One of
them wants a ship's mast mounted on his roof, and
another one needs a rock weighing half a ton, and
it has to be round. A person can find anything if he
takes the time, that is, if he can afford to look. And
while he's looking, he's free, and he finds things he
never expected. Sometimes people are very predict-
able: they want a kitten in June, for example, and

come the first of September they want someone to drown their cat. So someone does. But other times, people have dreams and want things they can keep.

Eriksson was the man who fulfilled these dreams. No one knew exactly what he found for himself along the way—probably a lot less than people thought. But he went on doing it anyway, perhaps for the sake of the search.

One of the mysterious and attractive things about Eriksson was that he didn't talk about himself. He never seemed to feel the urge. Nor did he talk about other people; they didn't interest him very much. His infrequent visits might occur at any time of the day or night, and they never lasted long. Depending on when he arrived, he might have a cup of coffee or a meal or even take a drink just to be polite, but then he would turn quiet and uneasy, he would start listening, and then he would leave. But as long as he stayed, he had everyone's undivided attention. No one did anything, no one looked at anything but Eriksson. They would hang on his every word, and when he was gone and nothing had actually been said, their thoughts would dwell gravely on what he had left unspoken.

He might pass by early in the morning and throw ashore a present—a small salmon or some cod, a wild rose with roots and soil in a paper carton or a nameplate that said "Captain's Cabin," a pretty metal box or a couple of glass floats with the glass-blower's mark. Many of these gifts were appreciated later in the form of trivial sums of money. It was the only chance the family had to try and put a price on their dreams. And dreams burn a lot of gasoline.

Sophia adored Eriksson. He never asked her what she did or how old she was. He greeted her just as solemnly as he greeted the others and said goodbye the same way—with a short nod and no smile. They would all go down to his boat to see him off. The boat was big and old and hard to start, but once it was running, it ran. He didn't take very good care of it. There was all sorts of trash washing around in the bilge water and the gunwale was cracked. But all the equipment was in good condition. He fried his fish on the engine block, and he slept in a sealskin sleeping bag the way his grandfather had done. Earth and seaweed and fish scales and sand went with him everywhere. He had his nets and decoys and his shotgun neatly arranged in the stern, but God only knew the significance of the sacks and boxes piled in the bow. He would slap the painter on board and shove off. The prop, which was used to rough treatment, would strike the shallow bottom several cheerful blows, and Eriksson would be off. He never waved as he headed out. His boat didn't have a name.

Just before midsummer, Eriksson landed at the island and heaved a box up on the rock. "It's some fireworks I picked up in a trade," he said. "I'll drop by on Midsummer Eve, if that's all right, and we'll see how they work." He kept the motor running while he talked, and then backed off as soon as he was through. The box was pretty damp, so they put it by the stove.

Midsummer became even more important than usual. Grandmother blacked and polished the stove and painted the stove doors silver. They washed all the windows and even the curtains. Naturally, no one thought Eriksson would notice—he never noticed anything indoors. But they cleaned the house anyway, just because he was coming. The day before the great event, they gathered birch and rowan and lilies-of-the-valley, and the mosquitoes were awful on the big islands in toward the mainland. They shook the aphids and the ants off in the sand and went back home. They turned the house into a green bower, inside and out. Every birch stood in its own pail of water. And because it was June, almost all of the wildflowers they had picked were white.

Grandmother wondered if they shouldn't have invited the relatives, but no one thought it would have been a good idea, not with Eriksson there. He was the kind of man who came alone and stayed that way until he figured it was time to leave.

In the morning, on Midsummer Eve, there was a strong wind from the north. Along toward noon, it started to rain, and Papa spread a tarpaulin over the bonfire they'd laid out on the point. The tarpaulin blew into the water, as it always did, so he took out a can of gasoline and put it behind a tree. It was a disgrace for a Midsummer bonfire not to burn. The day went slowly, and the wind did not let up. Papa worked at his desk. His launching platform for Eriksson's fireworks stood out on the veranda, with its cradles pointing upward at an angle.

They set the table for four. There would be herring and pork and potatoes, and two kinds of vegetables. And marinated pears for dessert.

"He doesn't eat dessert," said Sophia nervously. "And he doesn't eat vegetables, either. He calls it grass. You know that."

"Yes, I know," Grandmother said. "But it looks nice."

The aquavit was in the little cellar under the floor, and they had extra milk. Eriksson never drank more than one glass of aquavit, or maybe two—just for the sake of the occasion—but he did love milk.

"Take away the napkins," Sophia said. "They look dumb."

Grandmother took away the napkins.

The wind continued to blow piercingly all day, but it didn't increase. There was an occasional shower. The terns screamed out on the point, and evening came.

When I was young, in Sweden, Grandmother thought, the Midsummer weather was so different. Not a breeze, not a breath of wind. The garden was in bloom, and we had a maypole with garlands all the way up to the little banner at the top. But it was too bad that we never had any wind. We never had bonfires in Sweden. Why didn't we ever have a fire . . . She was lying on the bed staring up at the birch greenery, and after a while she fell asleep.

Suddenly someone shouted, and the door slammed. The room was quite dark, since no lamps can be lit on Midsummer. Grandmother sat up and realized that Eriksson must have arrived. "Hurry up!" Sophia shouted. "He doesn't want anything to eat! We have to get started right away. We're supposed to put on warm clothes and he's in a terrible rush!"

Grandmother staggered to her feet and found her sweater and her warm pants and her walking stick and at the last minute stuffed the Lupatro in her pocket. The others were running back and forth, and she could hear Eriksson's motor running down at the shore. It was lighter outside. The wind had gone over to the west and there was a fine, drizzling rain. Suddenly Grandmother was wide awake. She walked down to the water alone and climbed aboard. Eriksson didn't greet her. He was keeping a sharp watch out to sea, and not a word was spoken as they set off. Grandmother sat on the floor. As the boat moved along, she saw the rising and falling sea in brief glimpses over the railing, and she noticed the first Midsummer bonfires being lit along the coast to the north. There were not very many, and they were barely visible through the rain and fog.

Eriksson headed straight south for Outer Skerry. There were a lot of other boats going the same way. More and more of them appeared out of the darkness, like shadows. Wooden crates with a heavy load of lovely, rounded bottles were bobbing on the gray sea with only their upper edges showing black against the choppy water. Black, like the boats that sailed in at full speed, slowed down to haul the crates aboard, and then swept on again. The salvage went on like a neatly balanced dance. The Coast Guard were driving about in their powerful boats and salvaging what they could, turning a blind eye to everyone else. All the boats in the area were out at sea, ignoring one another. Eriksson held the rudder, and Sophia's father hung over the rail and lifted the crates on board. They stepped up the pace, cutting down on each motion so as not to lose a second, until finally they were working together in such perfect harmony with the moving

boat that it was a joy to watch. Grandmother
watched it, and appreciated and remembered. And
all the time, there seemed to be more and more of
this Midsummer bounty tossing in the waves
around the Gulf of Finland. Off toward the mainland, a few feeble rockets rose in the air, dreamers
shooting their arrows of light against the gray Midsummer sky. Sophia had fallen asleep.

Everything was salvaged, some by the right
hands and some by the wrong, but nothing was
simply lost. Along toward morning the makeshift
fleet split up. The boats floated farther and farther
apart, each one setting off by itself to its own home.
By dawn, the sea was empty. The wind died. The
rain stopped. A clear and lovely Midsummer morning arranged its colors in the sky, and it was very
cold. When Eriksson landed at the island, the terns
began to scream. He left the motor running and set
off again as soon as the others had climbed out.

For a while, it seemed to Papa that Eriksson
might have shared the booty, but that was a hasty,
passing thought. He made sandwiches for everyone and dragged Eriksson's box of fireworks out
onto the veranda. He put the rockets in their launching cradles. The first one wouldn't light, nor the
second. None of them would light; they had all been
ruined by the water. Only the very last one went off
and sailed up toward the sunrise in a shower of

blue stars. The terns started screaming again, and that was Midsummer.

Eriksson had sailed back south to make sure nothing had been missed.

The Tent

SOPHIA'S GRANDMOTHER had been a Scout leader when she was young, and, in fact, it was thanks to her that little girls were even allowed to be Scouts in those days. The girls never forgot what good times they had had, and they often wrote to Grandmother and reminded her of this or that incident, or quoted a verse of some song they used to sing around the campfire. It all seemed a little out of date to Grandmother now, and she thought the old girls were being just a bit sentimental, but she would think some friendly thoughts about them all the same. Then she'd think about how the Scouting movement had grown too large and lost its personal touch, and then she'd forget the whole thing. Grandmother's children had never been Scouts. No one had had the time, somehow, and it never came up.

One summer, Sophia's father bought a tent and

put it up in the ravine so he could hide there if too many people came. The tent was so small that you had to crawl in on all fours, but inside there was enough room for two if they lay close together. But no candles or lamps were allowed.

"Is it a Scout tent?" Sophia asked.

Grandmother snorted. "We sewed our own tents," she said, remembering what they had looked like—huge, sturdy, grayish-brown. This was a toy, a bright yellow plaything for veranda guests, and not worth having.

"Isn't it a Scout tent?" asked Sophia anxiously.

So her grandmother said maybe it was, after all, but a very modern one, and they crawled in and lay down side by side.

"Now you're not allowed to go to sleep," Sophia said. "You have to tell me what it was like to be a Scout and all the things you did."

A very long time ago, Grandmother had wanted to tell about all the things they did, but no one had bothered to ask. And now she had lost the urge.

"We had campfires," she answered briefly, and suddenly she felt sad.

"And what else?"

"There was a log that burned for a long time. We sat around the fire. It was cold out. We ate soup."

That's strange, Grandmother thought. I can't

describe things any more. I can't find the words, or maybe it's just that I'm not trying hard enough. It was such a long time ago. No one here was even born. And unless I tell it because I want to, it's as if it never happened; it gets closed off and then it's lost. She sat up and said, "Some days I can't remember very well. But sometime you ought to try and sleep in a tent all night."

Sophia carried her bedclothes to the tent. She closed the door to her little cottage and said goodbye as the sun went down. All by herself, she walked out to the ravine, which this evening had become an infinitely distant place, forsaken by God and man and Scout—a wilderness with an entire night ahead. She zipped shut the door of the tent and stretched out with the quilt up to her chin. The yellow tent glowed in the sunset, and suddenly it seemed very small and friendly. No one could look in and no one could look out; she was wrapped in a cocoon of light and silence. Just as the sun disappeared, the tent turned red and she fell asleep.

The nights were already long, and when Sophia woke up, there was nothing to see but the dark. A bird flew over the ravine and screamed, first close by and then once more far away. It was a windless night, yet she could hear the sea. And there was no one in the ravine, yet the gravel crunched as if under someone's foot. The sheltering tent had let in the night, as close as if she'd been sleeping on the open ground. More birds cried in various ways, and the darkness was filled with strange movements and sounds, the kind no one can trace or account for. The kind no one can even describe.

"Oh, dear God," Sophia said, "don't let me get scared!" And immediately she started thinking about what it would be like to get scared. "Oh, dear God, don't let them make fun of me if I *do* get scared!"

She really listened for the first time in her life. And when she got out in the ravine, she noticed for the first time what the ground really felt like under her toes and the soles of her feet. It was cold, grainy, terribly complicated ground that changed as she walked—gravel and wet grass and big flat stones, and every now and then some plant as high as a bush would brush against her legs. The ground was dark, but the sky had a faint, gray light. The island had grown tiny, floating on the water like a drifting leaf, but there was a light in the guest room window. Sophia knocked very gently, because every sound had become too large.

"How's it going?" Grandmother asked.

"Good," Sophia said. She sat on the foot of the bed and looked at the lamp and the nets and the raincoats hanging on the wall, and her teeth stopped chattering and she said, "There's no wind at all."

"No," said Grandmother. "It's quite calm."

Grandmother had two blankets. If you put one of them down on the rug and got a cushion, it would make a bed. It wouldn't be like going back to the cottage—it was almost like outdoors. No, it was indoors, it really was. But even if she wasn't out in the tent all alone, nevertheless, she had been. She had slept outdoors.

"So many birds tonight," Grandmother said.

There was another possibility: she could take a blanket and sleep on the veranda right next to the wall of the house. That would be outdoors *and* all alone. Oh, dear God!

"I couldn't sleep," Grandmother said, "and I got to thinking about sad things." She sat up in bed and reached for her cigarettes. Sophia handed her the matches automatically, but she was thinking about other things.

"You've got two blankets, don't you?" Sophia said.

"I mean it all seems to shrink up and glide away," Grandmother said. "And things that were a lot of fun don't mean anything any more. It makes me feel cheated, like what was the point? At least you ought to be able to talk about it."

Sophia was getting cold again. They had let her

sleep in a tent, even though she was too little to sleep in a tent. None of them knew what it was like, and they had just let her sleep in the ravine all by herself. "Oh is that so?" she said angrily. "What do you mean it's no fun?"

"Oh for heaven's sake," Grandmother said. "All I said was that when you're as old as I am, there are a lot of things you can't do any more . . ."

"That's not true! You do everything. You do the same things I do!"

"Wait a minute!" Grandmother said. She was very upset. "I'm not through! I know I do everything. I've been doing everything for an awfully long time, and I've seen and lived as hard as I could, and it's been unbelievable, I tell you, unbelievable. But now I have the feeling everything's gliding away from me, and I don't remember, and I don't care, and yet now is right when I need it!"

"What don't you remember?" asked Sophia anxiously.

"What it was like to sleep in a tent!" her grandmother shouted. She stubbed out her cigarette and lay down and stared at the ceiling. "In my country, in Sweden, girls had never been allowed to sleep in tents before," she said slowly. "I was the one who made it so they could, and it wasn't easy. We had a wonderful time, and now I can't even tell you what it was like."

The birds started screaming again—a big flock of them flew by, screaming steadily. The lamplight on the window made it look much darker outside than it really was.

"Well, I'll tell you what it's like," Sophia said. "You can hear everything much clearer, and the tent is very small." She thought for a moment and then went on. "It makes you feel very safe. And it's nice that you can hear everything."

"Yes," Grandmother said. "You can hear everything outside."

Sophia realized she was hungry and pulled the food box out from under the bed. They ate hard bread and sugar and cheese.

"I'm kind of sleepy," Sophia said, "so I think I'll go back now."

"Do," Grandmother said. She turned out the lamp, and after the initial darkness the room became lighter again and she could see everything distinctly. Sophia went out and closed the door. When she had gone, Grandmother rolled up in her blanket and tried to remember what it had been like. She could remember better now, much better, in fact. New images came back to her, more and more of them. It was cold in the first light, but she fell sound asleep in her own warmth.

The Neighbor

A BUSINESSMAN built a house on Blustergull Rock. At first, no one mentioned it. They had developed a habit, over the years, of not talking about painful things, in order to make them less painful. But they were very much aware of the house.

People who live on islands are always letting their eyes glide along the horizon. They see the lines and curves of the familiar skerries, and the channel markers that have always stood in the same spots, and they are strengthened in their calm awareness that the view is clear and everything is in its place. Now the view was no longer clear. It was broken by a big square house, a new and threatening landmark, a deep notch in the aspect of a horizon that had been their own for a very long time. The anonymous skerries that had been the island's threshold to the sea had acquired a strange new name and closed their lagoons. But worst of all, it was no longer the family who lived farthest out.

There was less than a mile between them and their new neighbor. The man was no doubt neighborly, too. It seemed very likely that he would love company and have a big family that would kick the moss off the rocks and play the radio and talk a lot. That sort of thing happened all the time, all over, farther and farther out from the mainland.

Early one morning, the workmen nailed on the tin roof—a huge, angry, glittering roof—under a cloud of screaming gulls and terns. The house was done, the men drove away in their boat, and there was nothing to do but wait for the arrival of the owner. But the days passed and he didn't come.

Toward the end of the week, Grandmother and Sophia took the dory out for a little row. When they came to the perch shallows, they decided to go on to Squire Skerry to look for seaweed, and once in the lagoon behind Squire Skerry, it was only a stroke of the oars to Blustergull Rock. There was no dock, only a big bank of gravel. In the middle of the gravel was a large sign with black letters that said PRIVATE PROPERTY—NO TRESPASSING.

"We'll go ashore," Grandmother said. She was very angry. Sophia looked frightened. "There's a big difference," her grandmother explained. "No well-bred person goes ashore on someone else's island when there's no one home. But if they put up a sign, then you do it anyway, because it's a slap in the face."

"Naturally," Sophia said, increasing her knowledge of life considerably. They tied up to the sign.

"What we are now doing," Grandmother said, "is a demonstration. We are showing our disapproval. Do you understand?"

"A demonstration," her grandchild repeated, adding, loyally, "This will never make a good harbor."

"No," Grandmother agreed. "And they have the door on the wrong side of the house. They'll never get it open in a southwester. And look at their water barrels. Ha-ha. Plastic, of course."

"Ha-ha," Sophia said. "Plastic, of course."

They went closer to the house and could feel how the island had changed. It was no longer wild. It had become lower, almost flat, and looked ordinary and embarrassed. The vegetation had not been disturbed; on the contrary, the owner had had broad catwalks built over the heather and the blueberry bushes. He had been very careful of the vegetation. The gray juniper bushes had not been cut down. But the island seemed flat all the same, because it should not have had a house. From up close, this way, the house was fairly low. On the elevations, it had probably been pretty. It would have been pretty anywhere, except here.

They went up on the terrace. Under the eaves he had put up a plaque with the name of the house:

VILLA BLUSTERGULL. It was fancily carved and re-
sembled one of those fluttering geographical desig-
nations that are found on old maps. Above the door
hung two brand-new ship's lanterns and a grappling
iron; on one side was a freshly painted red buoy,
and on the other a bunch of artistically arranged
glass floats.

"It's always like that at the beginning," Grandmother said. "I suppose he'll learn."

"Learn what?" Sophia said.

Grandmother thought for a moment and repeated, "He'll learn." She went up to the shutters
that nearly covered the wall and tried to peek in.
The shutters were locked with padlocks, and the
door was secured with something called "LockInc."
Grandmother produced her knife and opened the
screwdriver blade. The padlocks had brass screws
that were easily removed.

"Are we breaking in?" Sophia whispered.

"Well, what do *you* think?" her grandmother
answered. "But of course normally we would never
do such a thing." She opened one of the shutters and
looked in. It was a big room with a fireplace. In
front of the fireplace the owner had big rattan easy
chairs with a lot of pillows, and a thick glass table
with brightly colored labels under the glass. Sophia
thought the room was wonderful, but she didn't

dare say so. Full-rigged ship in storm, Grandmother observed, with gold frame. Maps, binocu-
lars, sextants, ship models, anemometers. A regular
maritime museum.

"He's got a big painting," said Sophia uncer-
tainly.

"Yes. Very big. Everything he has is big."

They sat down on the terrace with their backs
to the house and gazed out over the long island,
which at once seemed wild and lonely again.

"Anyway," Sophia said, "I'll bet he doesn't
know how to sink his trash. He doesn't know you
have to fill all the cans and bottles before you sink
them. And all his old garbage will wash ashore at
our place and get caught in our nets. And everything he's got is too big!"

They heard the motor for a long time without
listening. The sound came closer and became a
roar, then changed to a purr and stopped. And then
there was silence, a charged and terrifying silence.
Grandmother stood up as quickly as she could and
said, "Go look, but don't let them see you." Sophia
crept in under the aspens, and when she came back
she was pale. "It's him, it's him!" she whispered
frantically. "It's the owner!"

Grandmother stared wildly around her, took a
few steps in one direction and then a few steps back.
She was beside herself with terror. "Don't let him

see you," she kept repeating. "See what he's doing, but don't let him see you!"

Sophia crawled back in under the aspens on her stomach. The owner had a big mahogany boat with an antenna on the cabin, and he was poling it in toward land. On the foredeck stood a dog and a skinny boy dressed in white. They jumped ashore together.

"They found our boat," Sophia hissed. "They're coming!"

Grandmother headed for the middle of the island with short, rapid strides, her walking stick jabbing into the ground and kicking up moss and pebbles. She was as rigid as a board and said not a word. It was pure, primitive flight, but she couldn't think of anything better. Sophia leaped ahead, turned and came back, and ran around her in circles. The shame of being discovered on someone else's island was enormous. They had stooped to the unforgivable.

They reached the thicket on the far side of the island, and Sophia crawled in under the creeping pines and disappeared. "Hurry up!" she shrieked in terrible distress. "Hurry up! Crawl!" And Grandmother crawled in after her, blindly, without thinking. She was dizzy and not feeling well; it was never good for her to hurry. "This is perfectly ridiculous," she said.

"We have to," Sophia whispered. "When it gets dark, we'll sneak down to the boat and row home."

Grandmother inched in under a pine tree that tore at her hair. She was silent. After a while they heard barking.

"That's their bloodhound," Sophia breathed into Grandmother's ear. "Did I tell you they had a bloodhound with them?"

"No, you certainly did not," said Grandmother angrily. "And don't hiss in my ear. Things are bad enough as they are."

The barking came nearer. When the dog caught sight of them, the barking rose an octave. It was a small black dog, as fierce as it was frightened. Its whole body shook with mixed feelings.

"Nice doggy," said Grandmother soothingly. "Shut up, you little bastard!" She found a lump of sugar in her pocket and threw it, which made the dog utterly hysterical.

"Hello in there!" called the owner. He was down on all fours, peering in under the scrubby trees. "The dog won't hurt you! My name's Malander, and this is my son Christopher—we call him Tofer."

Grandmother crawled out and said, "This is my granddaughter, Sophia." She was being very dignified, picking pine needles out of her hair as discreetly as she could. The dog was trying to bite her walking stick. Mr. Malander explained that she only wanted to play, and that her name was Delilah. "Delilah wants you to throw your stick so she can fetch it—you know."

"Really?" said Grandmother. "You don't say."

The son had a skinny neck and long hair, and was making a formidable attempt to be superior. Sophia stared at him coldly. Mr. Malander offered Grandmother his arm, very politely, and they walked slowly back through the heather while he told them how he'd built his cottage in a simple, coastal style because that was the way he wanted it, and how a person was more in tune with himself when he lived close to nature, and how they were neighbors now, weren't they, because didn't they live on the next island in? Sophia glanced up, but her grandmother's face was impassive as she replied that they had lived on that island for forty-seven years. This made a great impression on Malander. His voice altered and he began to say something about the sea—how he loved it, how the sea is forever the sea—and then suddenly he was embarrassed and stopped talking. The son started whistling and dribbled a pine cone, soccer style, with his feet, all the way up to the terrace. There was the padlock, still on the bench, with the screws around it.

"Aha!" said young Malander. "Prowlers. Typical."

His father looked distressed. He poked at the padlock and said he never would have imagined such a thing from the coastal people, he had always admired the skerry folk . . .

"They were probably just curious," said Grandmother quickly. "You know, people get curious when a place is all closed up. That's not the way . . . It's much better to leave everything open, with the key on a nail, say . . ." She was getting confused, and Sophia went blood-red in the face.

They went into the house for a little refreshment, just to be neighborly. "Welcome to our home," said Tofer Malander. "*Après vous*." The big room filled with sunshine as one shutter after another was thrown open. Mr. Malander explained that it was a picture window, and asked them to sit down and make themselves comfortable while he went to get some drinks.

Grandmother sat down in one of the rattan chairs, and Sophia hung on its back and looked around furtively.

"Don't look so cross," Grandmother whispered. "This is socializing, and you have to learn how to do it."

Malander came back with bottles and glasses and put them on the table. "Cognac," he said. "And

whiskey. But I'm sure you'd rather have a lemonade."

"I'm very fond of cognac," Grandmother said.
"A small glass, and no water, thank you. Sophia?
What would you like?"

"The other!" Sophia hissed in her ear.

"Sophia would prefer a lemonade," Grandmother said, and thought: We've got to teach her
some manners. We've made a mistake. She has to
spend more time with people she doesn't like, before it's too late.

They toasted each other, and Malander asked
if the fishing was good this time of year.

Grandmother said only in nets. They got some
cod and perch and sometimes a whitefish, close to
shore. Malander explained that actually he didn't
like to fish. It was primitive, undisturbed nature he
liked; that is, wilderness and solitude in general.
The son was embarrassed and drove his hands down
into the pockets of his narrow pants as far as they
would go.

"Solitude," Grandmother said. "Yes, indeed.
That is a luxury."

"Uplifting," Malander said. "Don't you think?"

"Yes," Grandmother said. "But a person can
also find solitude with others, though it is more
difficult."

"No, no, of course," said Malander alertly and

somewhat vaguely, and there was a long silence.

"Sugar!" Sophia whispered. "It's sour!"

"My granddaughter would like to have some sugar in her drink," Grandmother said. And to Sophia she said, "Don't drape your hair on the back of my neck all the time. And sit down. And stop blowing in my ear."

Tofer Malander announced that he was going to do a little casting from the point, and he took down a rod and reel from the wall and left.

"I am also fond of lonely islands," Grandmother said rather loudly.

"He's only sixteen," Malander said.

Grandmother asked how many they were, and he answered five, plus friends and help and so forth. Suddenly he was depressed and suggested they have another drink.

"No, thank you," Grandmother said. "I think we'll be going now. That was very good cognac." On the way out she stopped to look at some seashells in the window, and Malander said, "I collect them for the children."

"I collect seashells myself," Grandmother said.

The dog was waiting outside and took a bite at Grandmother's walking stick. "Sophia," she said. "Throw something for the dog." The child threw a stick and the dog retrieved it instantly. "Good Delilah," Sophia said. If nothing else, she could apparently learn to remember names, which was also a valuable social grace.

Down at the shore, Malander told them there would be a dock, eventually, and Grandmother advised him to use rollers and a winch instead, since the ice would break up a dock, or else a dinghy and a buoy. And she thought: There I go again. I'm always such a busybody when I'm tired. Of course he'll try to build a dock. Everyone does. We did, too.

The oars had been stowed backward and got all tangled in the painter, and they were off to a jumpy, amateurish start. Malander followed along the shore as they rowed out, all the way to the point, and from there he waved to them with his handkerchief.

When they were out of hearing, Sophia shook her head and said, "Well, my, my."

"What do you mean, 'Well, my, my'?" Grandmother said. "He just wants to be left alone, but he doesn't know it yet."

"What do you mean?"

"And he'll build his dock anyway."

"How do you know?"

"My dear child," said Grandmother impatiently, "every human being has to make his own mistakes." She was very tired, and wanted to get home. The visit had made her sad, somehow. Malander had an idea and was trying to work it out, but it would take him time. Sometimes people never saw things clearly until it was too late and they no longer had the strength to start again. Or else they forgot their idea along the way and didn't even realize that they had forgotten. As Grandmother rowed home, she gazed at the big house interrupting the horizon, and it seemed to her it looked like a channel marker. If you squinted and thought about something else, it might almost *be* a channel marker—an objective indicator that here was a change of course.

Every time there was a storm, they thought about Malander and tried to figure out different ways to save his boat. He never returned their visit, and so his house became an always fascinating landmark to consider and reflect upon.

The Robe

SOPHIA'S FATHER had a special bathrobe that he loved. It reached all the way to his feet and was made of very thick, stiff flannel that salt water, soil, and time had rendered even stiffer. The robe was probably German, originally, and had once been green. On its front, it still bore the remains of an intricate system of laces, along with a couple of large dark amber buttons. Thrown wide open, the robe was as broad as a tent.

In the beginning, when Papa was a young man, he used to sit out on the point in his bathrobe whenever it stormed and watch the waves. Later, it was nice to put on when he wanted to work or get warm, or simply hide.

The robe had survived various threats to its existence. There was the time some well-meaning relatives came out and, as a surprise, gave the island a good cleaning. They threw out a lot of things the family wanted, but, worst of all, they carried the bathrobe down to the water and let it float away. They claimed later that it smelled. Of course it smelled—that was part of its charm. Smell is important. It reminds a person of all the things he's been through; it is a sheath of memories and security. The robe smelled of good things, too—of smoke and the sea—but maybe they never noticed that. In any case, the robe came back. The wind blew, shifted, and reversed, the waves beat against the island, and one fine day they brought it home. After that, it smelled of seaweed, and Papa wore virtually nothing else that whole summer. Then there was the spring when they discovered a family of mice had been living in the robe. The collar was edged with a soft, downy material that the mice had nibbled off and used for bedclothes, along with some finely chewed handkerchiefs. And then one time Papa slept too close to the fire and the robe was scorched.

When Papa got a little older, he put the bathrobe up in the attic. He would go up there to think sometimes, and the others always took it for granted that he did his thinking in the robe. It lay under one of the little attic windows, long and dark and mysterious.

Sophia went through a rebellious phase one cold, rainy summer when being unhappy outdoors was a lot of trouble. So she would go up in the attic to be alone. She would sit in a cardboard box and stare at the robe, and she would say dreadful, crushing things, and it was hard for the robe to talk back.

In between times, she played cards with her grandmother. They both cheated shamelessly, and their card-playing afternoons always ended in a quarrel. This had never happened before. Grandmother tried to recall her own rebellious periods in order to try and understand, but all she could remember was an unusually well-behaved little girl. Wise as she was, she realized that people can postpone their rebellious phases until they're eighty-five years old, and she decided to keep an eye on herself. It rained constantly, and Papa worked from morning to night with his back to the room. They never knew if he was listening to them or not.

"Jesus," Sophia said. "There you sit with the King and you don't say anything!"

"Don't take the name of the Lord in vain," Grandmother said.

"I didn't say 'God,' I said 'Jesus.' "

"He's just as important as God is."

"He isn't either!"

"Of course he is!"

Sophia threw her cards on the floor and yelled, "I don't care about His old family! I hate families!" She clambered up the attic stairs and slammed the trapdoor behind her.

The attic was so low that there was only room to crawl. And if you didn't crawl carefully, you would hit your head on the rafters. It was also very crowded—just one narrow path through all the things being kept and saved and forgotten, all the things that had always been there and that not even the well-meaning relatives had found. The path led from the south window to the north window, and the roof betweeen the rafters was painted blue. Sophia had no flashlight, and it was dark. The path was an endless, empty street in the moonlight between shaggy houses. At the end of the street was the window with its moon-white sky, and beneath the window lay the robe, a pile of stiff folds, coal-black in its own shadow. Sophia had slammed the trapdoor with such a bang that she couldn't retreat. And so she crept over and sat down in her cardboard box. The bathrobe lay with one sleeve thrown forward across its gaping neck. She stared at it, and as she stared the sleeve rose just a trifle, and a tiny movement crept in under the robe and down toward the foot end. The folds altered imperceptibly, and the robe was still again. But she had seen it. There, inside the robe, there was something alive—or else the whole robe was alive. Sophia resorted to the simplest means of flight available in cases of great distress: she fell asleep. She was still asleep when they put her to bed, but in the morning she knew that there was danger in the robe. No one else must know. She kept the amazing truth to herself, and for several days she was almost elated. The rain had stopped. She drew pictures with shaggy shadows and made the moon very tiny, forgotten in a huge dark sky. She showed these pictures to no one. The danger dwelt in a fold deep down inside. It moved about at times and then crept back. When frightened, it showed its teeth, and it was far more dangerous than death.

Every day when the sun went down, Sophia would climb up the ladder, poke her nose through the trapdoor, and peer into the attic. She could see one little corner of the bathrobe if she craned her neck.

"What are you doing?" Grandmother asked.

"None of your business, nosey!" Sophia whined in her most irritating voice.

"Close the trapdoor. There's a draft," Grandmother said. "Go do something outside." She turned toward the wall and went on with her book. They had both become impossible and couldn't get along at all. They quarreled the wrong way. The days were cloudy, with rising winds, and Papa just sat at his desk and worked.

Sophia thought about the bathrobe more and more. The thing living in it was as quick as lightning but could lie in wait for days without moving. It could make itself thin and slide through a crack in the door, and then roll itself up again and crawl under the bed like a shadow. It didn't eat and never slept and hated everyone, most of all its own family. Sophia didn't eat either, that is, nothing but sandwiches.

It may not really have been her fault, but one day they ran out of bread and butter, and Papa took the boat in to the store to get supplies. He put the water jug in the boat, and the cans for kerosene and gasoline, and he took the shopping list from the wall and left. There was a southwest wind when he set out, and in a couple of hours it had risen so that the waves were riding right across the point. Grandmother tried to get the weather report on the radio, but she couldn't find the right button. She couldn't keep from going back to the north window every few minutes to look for him, and she didn't understand a word she read.

Sophia went down to the shore, and came back and sat down at the table. "And all you can do is just read," she said. She raised her voice and screamed, "You just read and read and read!" Then she threw herself down on the table and wept.

Grandmother sat up and said, "He'll make it all right." She was feeling a little ill and felt for the Lupatro behind the curtain. Sophia went on crying, but she kept an eye on Grandmother under her arm. "I don't feel good either," she screamed, and jumped up and vomited on the rug. Then she was quiet and pale and sat down on the bed.

"Lie down," Grandmother said, and she lay down. They both lay down and listened to the wind outside as it attacked in short, violent bursts.

"Once you get to the village," Grandmother said, "it always takes a long time at the store. There's always a line, and no one's in a hurry. And then the boy has to go down to the dock and fill you up with gasoline and kerosene. And you have to go pick up the mail, and sort through it to find what's

for you. And if there's a money order you have to
go in and get it stamped, and that means a cup of
coffee. And then he has to pay the bills. It can take
a long time."

"Go on," Sophia said.

"Well, then he has to take everything down to
the boat," Grandmother said. "He has to pack it all
in and cover it so it won't get wet. And on the way
down he remembers to pick some flowers, and give
some bread to the horse. And the bread's way down
at the bottom of a bag somewhere . . ."

"I shouldn't have eaten so many sandwiches!"
Sophia wailed and started to cry again. "I'm cold!"

Grandmother tried to cover her with a blanket,
but the child kicked it off and flailed her legs and
screamed that she hated all of them.

"Quiet!" Grandmother yelled. "Quiet down! Or
I'll throw up on you." Sophia stopped screaming
immediately. There was a moment's silence, and
then she said, "I want the bathrobe."

"But it's up in the attic," Grandmother said.

"I want it," her grandchild said.

And so Grandmother climbed the attic ladder.
It went fine. She crawled over to the window for the
robe and dragged it back to the trapdoor. Then she
dropped it down into the room and sat and rested
for a while, dangling her feet over the edge. She
hadn't been up there for a very long time, and she

read the labels on the boxes. String. Tackle. Bottles. All kinds of things. Rags and old trousers. She had printed the labels herself. They had painted the ceiling blue, but they hadn't put enough glue in the paint; it was flaking.

"What are you doing?" Sophia yelled. "Don't you feel good?"

"Yes," Grandmother answered through the trap. "I feel better." She lowered one leg very cautiously and found the step. Then she turned slowly over on her stomach and brought down the other leg.

"Take it easy!" Sophia called from down below. She saw Grandmother's stiff old legs move from one step to the next and finally reach the floor. Grandmother picked up the robe and came over to the bed.

"You have to shake it first," Sophia said. "And make it come out."

Grandmother didn't understand, but she shook the robe. It came slinking out one sleeve and disappeared under the door. The robe smelled the same as before. It was very heavy, and became a warm, dark cave. Sophia fell asleep right away, and Grandmother sat down in the north window to wait. It was blowing hard, and the sun was setting. She was far-sighted and saw the boat half an hour before it reached the island—a moustache of white foam that would appear at irregular intervals and sometimes vanish entirely.

When the boat reached the shelter of the island, she lay down on the bed and closed her eyes. A few minutes later, Sophia's father came into the room. He was wet through. He put down the bags and lit his pipe. Then he took the lamp and went out to fill it with kerosene.

The Enormous Plastic Sausage

SOPHIA KNEW that very small islands in the ocean have turf instead of soil. The turf is mixed with seaweed and sand and invaluable bird droppings, which is why everything grows so well among the rocks. For a few weeks every year, there are flowers in every crack in the granite, and their colors are brighter than anywhere else in the whole country. But the poor people who live on the green islands in toward the mainland have to make do with ordinary gardens, where they put their children to work pulling weeds and carrying water until they are bent with toil. A small island, on the other hand, takes care of itself. It drinks melting snow and spring rain and, finally, dew, and if there is a drought, the island waits for the next summer and grows its flowers then instead. The flowers are used to it, and wait quietly in their roots. There's no need to feel sorry for the flowers, Grandmother said.

The first to come up was the scurvywort, only an inch high, but vital to seamen who live on ship's biscuit. The second came up about ten days later in the lee of the channel marker, and it was called Stepmother, or love-in-idleness. Sophia and Grandmother used to walk out to see it. Sometimes it blossomed at the end of May and sometimes at the beginning of June. It had to be viewed at length. Sophia wondered why it was so important, and Grandmother said, "Because it's the first."

"No, it's the second," Sophia said.

"But it always comes up in the same place," Grandmother said. It occurred to Sophia that all of the others did, too, more or less, but she didn't say anything.

Every day, Grandmother would walk around the island in order to keep track of what was coming up. If she found a piece of uprooted moss, she would poke it back where it belonged. Since she had a hard time getting on her feet again whenever she sat down, Grandmother had become very skillful with her stick. She looked like an immense sand-piper as she walked slowly along on her stiff legs, stopping often to turn her head this way and that and have a look at everything before she moved on.

Grandmother was not always completely logical. Even though she knew there was no need to feel sorry for small islands, which can take care of themselves, she was very uneasy whenever there was a dry spell. In the evening she would make some excuse to go down to the marsh pond, where she had hidden a watering can under the alders, and she would scoop up the last bit of bottom water with a coffee cup. Then she would go around and splash a little water here and there on the plants she liked best, and then hide the can again. Every fall, she collected wild seeds in a matchbox, and the last day on the island she would go around and plant them, no one knew where.

The great change began with some flower catalogues that came for Sophia's father in the mail. For a while, he read nothing but flower catalogues, and finally he wrote to Holland and they sent him a box full of bags, and in each bag there was a brown-and-white bulb in a bed of light, protective down. Papa wrote for another box, and this time they sent him special gifts from Amsterdam: a porcelain wooden shoe that was really a vase, and several of the house bulbs, which were called something like Houet van

Moujk. Late that fall, Papa went back out to the island alone and planted his bulbs. And all winter he went on reading about plants and shrubs and trees in order to learn as much about them as he could. They were all of them delicate and pampered and had to be handled scientifically and with great care. They could not survive without real soil and water at specific times. They had to be covered in the fall so they wouldn't freeze, and uncovered in the spring so they wouldn't rot, and they had to be protected from field mice and storms and heat and frost—and the sea, of course. Papa knew all that, and perhaps that was why he was interested.

When the family returned to the island, they had two boats in tow. Huge bales of real black inland soil were rolled ashore and lay around near the water like sleeping elephants. Cartons and bags and baskets of plants wrapped in black plastic were carried up to the veranda, along with shrubs and whole trees with their roots in sacks, and hundreds of small peat pots full of delicate sprouts that would have to live indoors at first.

Spring was late, and there was sleet and storm every single day. They fed the fire until the stove shook, and they hung blankets in front of all the windows. They piled the suitcases against the wall and made narrow paths among the plants that stood huddled on the floor to keep warm. Occasionally,

Grandmother would lose her balance and sit down on some of them, but most of these straightened up again. They stacked firewood around the stove in rows to dry, and hung up their clothes from the rafters. And the poplar tree, the cement, and the shrubs were out on the veranda, under plastic. The storm continued, and by and by the sleet turned to rain.

Sophia's father woke up every morning at six o'clock. He built up the fire and made sandwiches for everyone and then went out. He tore up the turf in huge sheets and picked the bedrock clean. He dug deep holes all over the island and filled the ragged scars with real black soil. He collected stones and built walls to protect these gardens from the wind, he put up trellises on buildings and trees for the climbing plants, and he dug up the marsh pond in order to put in a concrete dike.

Grandmother stood in the window and watched. "The marsh will rise eight inches," she said. "The junipers won't like that."

"We're going to have speckled pond lilies and red water lilies in there," Sophia said. "Who cares what the junipers like?"

Her grandmother didn't answer. But she decided that when the weather got better she would rescue the broken turf and turn it right side up, because she knew it was full of daisies.

In the evenings, Papa would light his pipe and brood over the chemical composition of the soil. Flower catalogues covered the table and the bed, and the pictures shone gaudily in the lamplight. Sophia and Grandmother learned all the names and tested each other. They printed each of them on a slip of paper.

"*Fritillaria imperialis*," Sophia said. "*Forsythia spectabilis!* That's a lot more elegant than 'Stepmother.'"

"Oh, I don't know," Grandmother said. "For that matter, Stepmother's real name is *Viola tricolor*. Anyway, really elegant people don't need nameplates."

"Well, *we've* got a nameplate on our door in town," Sophia said, and they went on with their printing.

One night the wind died down and the rain stopped. The silence woke Grandmother, and she thought: Now he'll start planting.

The sunrise dazzled the house with light. There wasn't a cloud in the sky, and the sea and the island steamed. Sophia's father got dressed and went outside as quietly as he could. He took the plastic cover off the poplar and carried it down to its pit above the beach meadow. The poplar was twelve feet tall. Papa put soil around its roots and attached rope stays in every direction until it was very firmly braced. Then he carried the roses into the woods and laid them in the heather, and then he lit his pipe.

Once everything was in the earth, there was a long period of waiting. One still, warm day followed another. The Dutch bulbs opened their brown husks and grew straight up. Inside the dike, white root sprouts began moving in the slime, held in by a fine-meshed metal net that was anchored down with stones. New roots were seeking a foothold all over the island, and every stem and stalk was infused with life.

One morning, Sophia threw open the door and shouted, "Gudoshnik is coming up!"

Grandmother went out as fast as she could and put on her glasses. A slim, green spear was sticking up out of the earth, clearly and distinctly the beginning of a tulip. They studied it for a long time.

"It could be Dr. Plesman," Grandmother said. (But in fact it was Mrs. John T. Scheepers.)

Spring rewarded Papa's labors with great gentleness, and everything but the poplar began to grow. The buds swelled and burst into wrinkled, shiny leaves that quickly spread and enlarged. Only the poplar stood naked among its ropes and looked just the way it had when it arrived. The nice weather continued long into June, and there was no rain.

The whole island was covered with a system of plastic hoses that had already sunk halfway into the moss. The hoses were joined with brass couplings, and they all came together at a little pump that stood under a box beside the largest of the island's natural rainwater basins. There was a huge plastic cover over the basin to keep the water from evaporating. Everything had been worked out very cleverly. Twice a week, Papa started the pump, and the warm brown water ran through the hoses and sprinklers and splashed out over the ground in a fine spray or a thick stream, depending on the type of plant and its particular needs. Some were watered only one minute, others for three minutes, or five minutes, until Papa's egg timer rang and he turned off the precious supply. Obviously, he could not spare any water for the rest of the island, and it slowly turned brown. The island's own turf dried out and turned up its edges like slices of old sausage, several spruces died, and every morning the weather was just as relentlessly beautiful. In along the coast, thunderstorms ranged back and forth one after the other, with torrents of rain, but they never made it out to sea. The water in the big basin sank lower and lower. Sophia prayed to God, but it didn't

help. And then one evening while Papa was doing
the watering, the pump made a dreadful gurgling
noise and the hose went slack. The basin was completely empty, and the plastic cover stuck to the
bottom in a million wrinkled folds.

Sophia's father walked around thinking one
whole day. He made calculations and drew plans
and took the boat in to the store to use the phone. A
great heat wave settled over the island, which
looked more and more exhausted every day. Papa
went in to the store to use the phone again. Finally
he took the bus into town, and Sophia and Grandmother understood that the situation had become
catastrophic.

When Papa came back, he brought the enormous plastic sausage with him. It was the color of
old oranges, and its heavy folds filled half the boat.
It was specially constructed. There was clearly no
time to be lost, so the pump and the hoses were
loaded aboard and they set off immediately.

The sea lay glossy and listless in a shroud of
heat, and over the coast towered the usual wall of
deceitful clouds. The gulls barely lifted as they
drove by. It was a very important expedition. By
the time they reached Bog Skerry, the boat was so
hot the tar was running, and the plastic sausage
stank horribly. Papa carried the pump up to the
bog, which was large and deep and full of sedge and

cotton grass. He screwed the hoses together, heaved the sausage into shallow water, and started the pump. The hose filled and straightened out across the rock, and very, very slowly the plastic sausage began to grow. Everything went according to plan and expectation, but no one dared tempt fate by talking. It grew into a colossal, shiny balloon, an orange raincloud, ready to burst with the thousands of liters of water in its belly.

"Dear God, don't let it burst," Sophia prayed.

And it didn't. Papa turned off the pump and carried it down to the boat. He stowed away the hoses. He moored the sausage firmly to the stern and placed the family on the middle seat. Finally, he started the motor. The lines drew taut and the motor pulled, but the sausage didn't move. Papa went ashore and tried to push, but nothing happened.

"Dear God who loves little children," Sophia whispered, "please make it come loose."

Papa tried again and nothing happened. Then he took a run and threw himself at the plastic sausage and they both began to glide across the slippery sea grass and right on into the water in one long, gulping flow. And Sophia started to scream.

"Now don't blame God," said Grandmother, who was very interested in the whole procedure.

Sophia's father climbed into the boat and started the motor with a jerk. The boat took a leap forward, pulling Sophia and Grandmother off their seat, and the enormous plastic sausage sank slowly down into the water, straining at its lines. Papa hung over the stern and tried to see what it was doing. It crept through the seaweed, and where the bay deepened it disappeared completely and pulled the motor down into the water until it spit. The family shifted their weight quickly forward: there was less than four inches from the gunwales to the water.

"I'm not going to pray to Him again," said Sophia angrily.

"He knows, anyway," said Grandmother, who was lying on her back in the bow. The thing about God, she thought, is that He usually does help, but not until you've made an effort on your own.

The plastic sausage glided slowly along in the green depths where the shadow of the sea begins, a great bubble of living water. Everyone knows that rain water is lighter than salt water, but in this case, the pump had sucked in a lot of mud and sand. It was very hot in the boat, and there was a smell of gasoline. The motor was working like mad. Grandmother fell asleep. The sea was as glossy as ever, and the banks of clouds had piled up high above the coast. The enormous plastic sausage rose leisurely over a reef and bounced down on the other side. The motor raced and the boat sped up and then jerked back again and took in water over the stern. And then it moved on again, but very slowly. Grandmother started snoring. A hard, dry clap of thunder rolled out between the islands, and black breezes sprang out across the water and then vanished. As they rounded the long point, there came a second thunderclap, just as the plastic sausage slid over another reef. Grandmother woke up. She saw a short, glassy wave pour in over the stern, and she realized she was wet. The air had cooled off a little. Confused puffs of clouds were racing across the sky, and the water in the boat felt warm and pleasant. The landscape had grown darker, the shallows glowed bright yellow, and it smelled of rain. They drove slowly in toward the island while the storm laid its shadow over the sea, and all three of them sat silent and breathless in that state of uncertainty that so rarely seems exciting at the time. It was shallower here, and every time the plastic sausage struck bottom, the water level rose in the boat, until finally the sea was pouring in steadily over the railing. And just then came another clap of thunder.

Papa undid the sputtering motor and waded ashore, and Sophia followed him with the hose. Very carefully, Grandmother rolled over the side and started to wade, occasionally swimming a couple of strokes just to remember what it felt like. Then she sat down on the rock and poured the water out of her shoes. The bay was full of small, angry waves, and the plastic sausage glowed beneath the surface like an apricot from Paradise. Papa dragged and hauled, and very slowly it lifted its bright orange stomach and its brass navel toward the sky. He connected the hoses and started the pump, and a big clump of mud and sand flew straight up into the air. And after that, a stream of water slammed against the rock and sent the moss flying. "Water! Water!" Sophia screamed, soaking wet and a little hysterical. She clasped the pulsing hose to her chest and felt it pumping water for Clematis, Nelly Moser, Freesia, Fritillaria, Othello, and Madame Droutschki, for Rhododendron and *Forsythia spectabilis*. She saw the powerful stream of water arch in over the island and down into the dry basin. "Water!" Sophia roared, and she ran to the poplar and saw what she had expected to see—a green root sprout. And in the same instant, the rain came, warm and tumultuous, and the island was doubly blessed.

Grandmother had had to be frugal all her life, and so she had a weakness for extravagance. She watched the basin and the barrels and every crevice in the granite fill with water and overflow. She looked at the mattresses out being aired and the dishes that were washing themselves. She sighed contentedly, and, absorbed in thought, she filled a coffee cup with precious drinking water and poured it over a daisy.

The Crooks

ONE STILL, warm August night there came a ringing trumpet blast from out at sea—like Gabriel blowing his horn. A double row of lights came gliding in toward the island in a slow curve. It was a huge yacht, purring as only very expensive and very fast boats can purr, and carrying lights of every color from dark blue and blood-red to white. The whole ocean held its breath. Sophia and her grandmother stood out on the granite in their nightgowns and watched. The strange boat slid closer and closer, with its motor throttled down and its lights reflecting in the water like dancing snakes of fire. Then it disappeared behind the island. Sophia's father had put on his pants, and he ran out to meet it. For a long time there was perfect silence, and then faint music floated toward them from across the island.

"They're having a party," Sophia whispered. "Let's go, too. Let's get dressed and go over right now!"

But Grandmother said, "Wait a bit. Wait till he comes to get us."

They lay down in their beds while they waited, and pretty soon they fell asleep. And the next morning the boat was gone. It had sailed away.

Sophia threw herself down on the rock and wept. "He could have come to get us!" she wailed. "He let us sleep and they were having a party; I'll never forgive him!"

"He behaved very badly," said Grandmother sternly. "And I'll tell him so when he wakes up."

The image of the mysterious boat returned to overwhelm Sophia and she screamed with grief.

"Blow your nose," her grandmother said. "It was a dreadful disappointment, but blow your nose anyway. You look awful." She waited a moment and said, "I'll bet they were very unpleasant people. They only inherited the boat. They don't know a thing about boats. But," she added vindictively, "they did do the interior decorating themselves, and the colors are awful."

"You really think?" moaned Sophia, sitting up.

"Awful," her grandmother assured her. "They've got shiny silk curtains that are brown and gold and puce, and they've got standing lamps and plastic plates and paintings on velvet—humorous ones, which makes it worse . . ."

"Okay, okay," said Sophia impatiently. "Go on."

"And if someone hadn't given them the boat they would have stolen it."

"Who from?"

"From a poor smuggler. And they stole all his contraband, too, every bit of it, and they only drink pop themselves. They only took it for the money," Grandmother went on, warming to her subject. "And they went off without a map and without any oars!"

"But why did they come to our place?"

"So they could hide everything in the ravine and then come back and get it later."

"Do you believe all that?"

"Some of it," said Grandmother cautiously.

Sophia stood up and blew her nose. "Now," she said. "Now I'll tell you what happened last night. You sit down and listen. When Papa came down to their boat, they wanted him to buy a bottle of ninety-six proof, and it was really expensive. Now you be Papa. Say what he said."

"He said, very proudly, 'It's beneath my dignity to buy ninety-six proof. I'll find my own liquor if I want some, salvage it from the sea at the risk of my life. So keep your precious rotgut, my dear sir.

What's more, my family doesn't like the taste.' Now it's your turn."

" 'Oh indeed? So you have a family, sir? And where is this family of yours, pray tell?' "

" 'Nowhere nearby.' "

"But we were right here all the time!" Sophia shouted. "Why didn't he say we were here?"

"To spare us."

"Why? Why do we have to be spared whenever something happens? That's not the truth. We didn't have to be spared if they were playing dance music!"

"They had the radio on," Grandmother said. "Just the radio. They were waiting for the weather and the news—to find out if the police were after them."

"You can't fool me!" Sophia shouted. "There isn't any news at one o'clock in the morning. They were having a party and having fun, and we missed it!"

"Have it your own way," Grandmother said angrily. "They had a party and a lot of fun. But we don't go to parties with just anyone."

"I do," said Sophia defiantly. "I go to parties with just anyone, as long as I can dance! Papa and I both do!"

"Well, then, go ahead," Grandmother said, and

started to walk away along the shore. "Go to a party with crooks if you want. As long as your legs hold out—that's the main thing. You don't care about anything else."

The boat had thrown its garbage overboard, expensive garbage that showed exactly what they'd been doing. Most of it had washed up on the rocks.

"Orange peels and candy wrappers. And crayfish!" said Sophia with emphasis.

"Crooks are famous for eating crayfish," Grandmother observed. "Didn't you know that?" She was tired of the whole business and had a feeling the conversation should have been used for some more instructive purpose. And, for that matter, why shouldn't crooks eat crayfish?

"You're saying the wrong thing," Sophia said. "Now, think for a minute. I was saying that Papa had a crayfish party with the crooks and forgot about us. That was how the whole thing started."

"Yes, yes, yes," Grandmother said. "Make up something for yourself then, if you don't believe my story."

An empty bottle of Old Smuggler was bumping gently against a rock. It was quite possible that he hadn't forgotten at all, that he just thought it was nice to be on his own. Perfectly understandable, actually.

"*Now* I know," Sophia burst out. "They gave

him a sleeping potion. Just when he was about to
go get us, they put a pinch of sleeping powder in
his glass, and that's why he's sleeping so late!"

"Nembutal," Grandmother suggested. Grandmother liked to sleep. Sophia stared at her with
wide-open eyes. "Don't say that!" she screamed.
"What if he never wakes up!" She turned around
and started to run. She was crying out loud in terror, and she turned and jumped and started running, and right then, right there, on top of a rock,
held down with a stone, was a huge box of chocolates. It was a great big pink-and-green package
tied with silver ribbon. The bright colors made the
rest of the island look grayer than ever, and there
was no doubt that the wonderful box was a present.
There was a little card inside the bow. Grandmother put on her glasses and read it to herself.
"Love and kisses to those too old and too young
to come to the party." "How tactless!" she muttered through her teeth.

"What does it say? What did they write?" Sophia shouted.

"It says," her grandmother said, "what it says
is: 'We have behaved very badly, and it's all our
fault. Forgive us if you can.'"

"Can we?" Sophia asked.

"No," said Grandmother.

"Yes. We ought to forgive them. In fact, you

should always forgive crooks. How nice they really *were* crooks after all. Do you think the chocolates are poisoned?"

"No, I don't think so. And that sleeping powder was probably pretty weak."

"Poor Papa," Sophia sighed. "He just barely escaped."

And indeed he had. He had a headache all day long and could neither eat nor work.

The Visitor

SOPHIA'S FATHER emptied the grounds from the coffee pot and carried the flowerpots out to the veranda.

"What's he doing that for?" Grandmother asked, and Sophia said the plants would be better off outdoors while he was gone.

"What do you mean, 'gone'?" Grandmother asked.

"For a whole week," Sophia said. "And we're going to stay with some people on one of the inner islands till he gets back."

"I didn't know that," Grandmother said. "No

one told me." She went into the guest room and tried to read. Of course, you moved a potted plant to wherever it would get on best. It would do fine on the veranda for a week. If you were going to be gone longer than that, you had to leave it with someone who could water it. It was a nuisance. Even potted plants got to be a responsibility, like everything else you took care of that couldn't make decisions for itself.

"Come and eat!" Sophia called from outside the door.

"I'm not hungry," Grandmother said.

"Don't you feel good?"

"No," Grandmother said.

The wind blew and blew. The wind was always blowing on this island, from one direction or another. A sanctuary for someone with work to do, a wild garden for someone growing up, but otherwise just days on top of days, and passing time.

"Are you mad?" Sophia said, but her grandmother didn't answer. The Övergårds came by with the mail, and Papa found out he didn't have to go into town after all. "Oh, good," Sophia said, but Grandmother didn't say a word. She became very quiet and no longer made bark boats, and when she did the dishes or cleaned fish, she didn't look as if she enjoyed it. And on nice mornings she no longer sat in the woodyard and combed her hair, slowly, with her face turned toward the sun. She just read, and didn't even care how the books came out.

"Can you make kites?" Sophia said, but Grandmother said she could not. As the days went by, they became strangers to each other, with a shyness that was almost hostile.

"Is it true you were born in the eighteen-hundreds?" Sophia yelled through the window.

"What of it?" Grandmother answered, very distinctly. "What do you know about the eighteen-hundreds?"

"Nothing, and I'm not interested, either," Sophia shouted and ran away.

The island was blessed with mild night rain. A lot of lumber drifted by and was salvaged. No one came to visit, and there was no mail. An orchid bloomed. Everything was fine, and yet everything was overshadowed by a great sadness. It was August, and the weather was sometimes stormy and sometimes nice, but for Grandmother, no matter what happened, it was only time on top of time, since everything is vanity and a chasing after the wind. Papa did nothing but work at his desk.

One evening, Sophia wrote a letter and stuck it under the door. It said, "I hate you. With warm personal wishes, Sophia."

All the words were correctly spelled.

Sophia made a kite. The directions were in a newspaper she found in the attic, but even though she did exactly what it said, the kite did not turn out. The tape wouldn't stick and the tissue paper tore and the paste got in all the wrong places. When the kite was finished, it refused to fly and kept slamming into the ground as if it wanted to destroy itself, and finally it threw itself in the marsh. Sophia put it outside Grandmother's door and went away.

What a smart little girl, Grandmother thought. She knows that sooner or later I'll make her a kite that can fly, but that doesn't help. That doesn't matter at all.

One calm day, a little white boat with an outboard motor approached the island. "It's Verner," Grandmother said. "He's back with another bottle of sherry." For a while she considered being ill, but she changed her mind and went down to meet him.

Verner was looking very dapper, with a linen hat. The boat was obviously from the inner islands, but it made an attempt to be sporty. It had a hogged keel. Verner declined assistance and came toward her with his arms spread wide and called out, "Dear old friend, are you still alive?"

"As you can see," said Grandmother dryly, allowing herself to be embraced. She thanked him for the bottle, and he said, "You see that I remember. It's the same sherry I brought in nineteen-ten."

How silly, she thought. Why could I never bring myself to tell him I hate sherry? And now it's too late. It really was a shame, seeing that she had now reached the age where a person can safely be truthful about small things.

They took some perch from the live box and ate a little earlier than usual. "Skoal," said Verner gravely, and turned toward Grandmother. "To the final landscape of our old age, as summer fades. This is a fine moment. Silence settles around us, each of us wanders his own way, and yet we all meet by the sea in the peaceful sunset."

They took tiny sips of their sherry.

"I suppose," Grandmother said. "But they did promise a breeze for tonight. How much horsepower does your motor have?"

"Three," Sophia guessed.

"Four and a half," said Verner curtly. He took a piece of cheese and looked out the window.

Grandmother could see that his feelings were hurt. She tried to be as nice as she could through coffee, and then she suggested the two of them go for a walk. They took the path to the potato patch, and she remembered to lean on his arm every time the ground was uneven. It was very warm and still.

"How are your legs?" Verner asked.

"Bad," said Grandmother heartily. "But sometimes they seem to work all right." And she asked him what he was doing these days.

"Oh, a little of everything." He was still offended. Suddenly he burst out, "And now Backmansson is gone."

"Where did he go?"

"He is no longer among us," Verner explained angrily.

"Oh, you mean he's dead," said Grandmother. She started thinking about all the euphemisms for death, all the anxious taboos that had always fascinated her. It was too bad you could never have an intelligent discussion on the subject. People were either too young or too old, or else they didn't have time.

Now he was talking about someone else who was gone, and about the clerk at the store, who was so unfriendly. They were building such ugly houses everywhere, and people went ashore on other people's land without so much as a by-your-leave, but of course there had to be progress.

"Oh, stuff and nonsense," Grandmother said. She stopped and turned to face him. "Just because more and more people do the same dumb things, that's nothing to make such a fuss about. Progress is another thing entirely, you know that. Changes. Big changes."

"My dear," said Verner quickly, "I know what you're going to say. Forgive me for interrupting, but you're about to ask me if I never read the papers."

"Not at all!" Grandmother exclaimed, very much hurt. "All I'm asking you is, don't you ever get curious? Or upset? Or simply terrified?"

"No, I really don't," Verner replied frankly. "Though I guess I've had my share of upset." His eyes were troubled. "You're so hard to please. Why do you use such harsh words? I was only telling you the news."

They walked by the potato patch and came down to the meadow by the shore. "That's a real poplar," said Grandmother, to change the subject. "It's taking root, look there. A friend of ours brought some genuine swan droppings from Lapland, and it liked them."

"Taking root," Verner repeated. He was silent for a moment and then went on. "It must be a great comfort to you to live with your granddaughter."

"Stop that," Grandmother said. "Stop talking in symbols, it's old-fashioned. I talk about taking root and right away you're into grandchildren. Why do you use so many euphemisms and metaphors? Are you afraid?"

"My dear old friend," said Verner, greatly distressed.

"I'm sorry," Grandmother said. "It's really a kind of politeness; I'm trying to show you I take you seriously."

"It is clearly an effort," said Verner gently. "You should be a little more careful with your compliments."

"You're right," Grandmother said.

They walked on toward the point in peaceful silence. Finally, Verner said, "Years ago you never talked about horsepower and fertilizer."

"I didn't realize they were interesting. Commonplace things can be fascinating."

"But yourself, personal things—you don't talk about that," Verner observed.

"Maybe not about the things that matter most," Grandmother said. She stopped to think. "In any case, less than I used to. I suppose I've already said most of it by this time. And I realized that it wasn't worth it. Or that I didn't have the right to say it."

Verner was silent.

"Do you have any matches?" she asked. He lit her cigarette, and they turned back toward the house. There was still no wind.

"It isn't my boat," he said.

"I didn't think it was. It has a hogged keel, too. Did you borrow it?"

"I just took it," Verner said. "I took it and drove off. It's very unpleasant to have them worry about you all the time."

"But you're only seventy-five," said Grandmother in astonishment. "Surely you can do what you like."

"It's not that easy," Verner replied. "You have to be considerate. They do have a certain responsibility for you, after all. And when you get right down to it, you are mostly just in the way."

Grandmother stopped and poked at a piece of moss with her walking stick. She got it back in place and walked on.

"Sometimes I get very depressed," Verner said. "You said a person shouldn't talk about the things that matter most, and here I am doing it anyway. I always seem to say the wrong thing today."

The sea was yellow in the evening light, and perfectly calm.

"Do you mind if I smoke?" he said.

"Please do, Verner," she said.

Verner lit a little cigar. "They talk about hobbies all the time," he said. "You know—a hobby."

"Yes," Grandmother said. "You're supposed to want one."

"Collecting things!" Verner went on. "It's so stupid. I would like to make things. With my hands, you know. But I'm not very good at that sort of thing."

"But you could make things grow!"

"Exactly!" Verner exclaimed. "You're just the same, just exactly. 'Why don't you have a garden?' they're always saying. 'Watch things grow!' I might have thought of that for myself, if only they hadn't said anything."

"Yes, you're quite right about that," Grandmother said. "It's true. You have to come to it by yourself."

They fetched his basket and his sweater, and everyone said goodbye. Grandmother proposed a glass of sherry, but Verner explained that sherry was a drink he had never really liked but only valued in conjunction with the memories they shared, which were very dear to him.

"They are dear to me, too," said Grandmother honestly. "Now set a course straight past the Horse Rocks, it's deep the whole way. And try to think of some way to outwit them."

"I will," Verner said. "I promise you." He started the motor and headed straight for home.

"Who's he going to outwit?" Sophia asked.

"Relatives," Grandmother said. "Nasty relatives. They tell him what to do without asking him what he wants, and so there's nothing at all he really does want."

"How awful!" Sophia cried. "That would never happen with us!"

"No, never!" Grandmother said.

Of Angleworms and Others

ONE SUMMER, Sophia was suddenly afraid of small animals, and the smaller they were, the more afraid she was. This was altogether new. Ever since the first time she trapped a spider in a matchbox in order to make it a pet, her summers had been full of caterpillars, tadpoles, worms, beetles, and similar uncompanionable creatures, whom she provided with everything they could want from life, including, eventually, their freedom. Now everything was changed. She walked about with cautious, anxious steps, staring constantly at the ground, on the look-out for things that crept and crawled. Bushes were dangerous, and so were sea grass and rain water. There were little animals everywhere. They could turn up between the covers of a book, flattened and dead, for the fact is that creeping animals, tattered animals, and dead animals are with us all our lives, from beginning to end. Grandmother tried to discuss this with her, to no avail. Irrational terror is so hard to deal with.

One morning, they found a strange bulb washed ashore on the sand. They decided to plant it outside the guest room. Sophia put her spade in the ground to make a hole, the spade cut an angleworm in two, and when she saw the two halves writhing on the black earth, she threw down the spade, backed up against the wall of the house, and screamed.

"They'll grow out again," Grandmother said. "They really will. They'll grow out again. It's all right, believe me." She continued to talk about angleworms as she planted the bulb. Sophia calmed down, but she was still very pale. She sat silently on the veranda steps with her arms around her knees.

"You know," Grandmother said, "I don't think anyone's ever taken a sufficient interest in angleworms. Someone who's really interested ought to write a book about them."

That evening, Sophia asked whether "some" was spelled with an *o* or a *u*.

"*O*," said Grandmother.

"I'll never get anywhere with this book," said Sophia angrily. "How can I think if I have to worry about spelling all the time? I lose my place, and the whole thing's a mess!" The book consisted of a lot of blank pages sewn together at the spine. She threw it on the floor.

"What's it called?" Grandmother asked.

"*A Study of Angleworms That Have Come Apart*. But I'll never get it written!"

"Sit down somewhere and dictate," Grandmother said. "I'll do the writing, and you tell me what to write. We've got lots of time. Now where did I put my glasses?"

It was a particularly good evening to begin a book. The setting sun threw plenty of light through the window, and Grandmother opened to the first page, which already carried an illustration of an angleworm in two parts. The guest room was cool and quiet, and Papa sat working at his desk on the other side of the wall.

"I like it when he's working," Sophia said. "I always know he's there. Read what I wrote."

" 'Chapter One,' " Grandmother read. " 'Some people fish with worms.' "

"Space," Sophia said. "Now go on: I won't say what their names are, but it's not Papa. Now take your scared worm—it will pull itself together to . . . How much does it pull itself together?"

"To, say, one-seventh of its length."

"To, say, one-seventh of its length, which makes

it little and fat and easy to stick a hook through, which is not what it had in mind. But now take your smart worm. It makes itself as long as it can so there's nothing to stick a hook through, and then it comes apart. Science does not yet know if it just breaks, or if the worm is being clever, because you can't always tell, but . . ."

"Wait a minute," Grandmother said. "How about if I put '. . . whether this is from over-stretching or shows real intelligence'?"

"Put anything you want," said Sophia impatiently. "Just so they'll understand. Now don't interrupt. It goes on like this: The worm probably knows that if it comes apart, both halves will start growing separately. Space. But we don't know how much it hurts. And we don't know, either, if the worm is afraid it's going to hurt. But anyway, it does have a feeling that something sharp is getting closer and closer all the time. This is instinct. And I can tell you this much, it's no fair to say it's too little, or it only has a digestive canal, and so that's why it doesn't hurt. I am sure it does hurt, but maybe only for a second. Now take the smart worm that made itself long and came apart in the middle, that may have been like pulling a tooth, for example, except it didn't hurt. When it had calmed its nerves, it could tell right away it was shorter, and then it saw the other half right beside it. Let

me make this a little easier to understand by putting
it this way: Both halves fell down on the ground,
and the person with the hook went away. They
couldn't grow back together, because they were terribly upset, and then, of course, they didn't stop to
think, either. And they knew that by and by they'd
grow out again, both of them. I think they looked
at each other, and thought they looked awful, and
then crawled away from each other as fast as they
could. Then they started to think. They realized
that from now on life would be quite different, but
they didn't know how, that is, in what way."

Sophia lay down on the bed and stared at the
ceiling and thought. It was getting dark in the
guest room, and Grandmother got up to light the
lamp.

"Don't," Sophia said. "Don't light the lamp. Use
a flashlight. Listen, is 'presumably' right?"

"Yes," Grandmother said. She turned on the
flashlight and put it down on the night table and
waited.

"Presumably, everything that happened to them
after that only seemed like half as much, but this
was also sort of a relief, and then, too, nothing they
did was their fault any more, somehow. They just
blamed each other. Or else they'd say that after a
thing like that, you just weren't yourself any more.
There is one thing that makes it more complicated,

and that is that there is such a big difference between the front end and the back end. A worm
never goes backwards, and so for that reason, it has
its head only at one end. But if God made angleworms so they can come apart and then grow out
again, why, there must be some sort of secret nerve
that leads out in the back end so that later on it
can think. Otherwise it couldn't get along by itself.
But the back end has a very tiny brain. It can probably remember its other half, which went first and
made all the decisions. And so now," said Sophia,
sitting up, "now the back end says, 'Which way
should I grow out? Should I make a new tail, or
should I make a new head? Should I go on following and never have to make any important decisions, or should I be the one who always knows
best, until I come apart again? That would be exciting.' But maybe he's so used to being the tail
that he just lets things go on the way they are.
Did you write everything I said?"

"Every word," Grandmother said.

"Now comes the end of the chapter: But maybe
the front end thinks it's nice not having anything
to drag around behind it, but who knows, because
it's hard to tell. Nothing is easy when you might
come apart in the middle at any moment. But no
matter what you think, you should never fish with
worms."

"There," said Grandmother. "End of book, and the end of the paper, too."

"That's not the end at all," Sophia said. "Now comes Chapter Two. But I'll work on that tomorrow. How do you think it sounds?"

"Very persuasive."

"I think so, too," Sophia said. "Maybe people will learn something from it."

They continued the following evening under the heading "Other Pitiful Animals."

"Small animals are a great problem. I wish God had never created small animals, or else that He had made them so they could talk, or else that He'd given them better faces. Space. Take moths. They fly at the lamp and burn themselves, and then they fly right back again. It can't be instinct, because that isn't the way it works. They just don't understand, so they go right on doing it. Then they lie on their backs and all their legs quiver, and then they're dead. Did you get all that? Does it sound good?"

"Very good," Grandmother said.

Sophia stood up and shouted, "Say this: say I hate everything that dies slow! Say I hate everything that won't let you help! Did you write that?"

"Yes, I've got it."

"Now come daddy-longlegs. I do a lot of thinking about daddy-longlegs. You can't ever help them without breaking two of their legs. No, write three of their legs. Why can't they pull in their legs? Write: When little kids bite the dentist, it's the dentist who gets hurt. Wait a minute." Sophia thought for a moment with her face in her hands. "Write 'Fish,' " she said. "And then a space. Little fish die slower than big fish, and yet people aren't nearly as careful about the little fish. They let them lie around on the rocks for a long time and breathe air, and that's like holding somebody's head under water. And the cat . . ." Sophia went on. "How do you know it starts from the head? Why don't you make sure the fish are dead? The cat might be tired, and maybe the fish doesn't taste good, and so it starts from the tail, and that makes me scream! And I scream when you salt them, and when the water's so hot it makes them jump! I won't eat fish like that, and it serves you right!"

"You dictate too fast," Grandmother said. "Shall I put 'it serves you right!'?"

"No," Sophia said. "This is a book. Stop after 'it makes them jump.' " She was silent for a while, and then she went on. "Chapter Three. Space. I will eat crayfish, but I don't want to watch when they're cooking them, because crayfish are awful when they're being cooked, so you have to be very careful."

"That's true," said Grandmother, and giggled.

"Jesus," Sophia burst out. "This is serious. Don't say anything. Write: I hate field mice. No. Write: I hate field mice, but I don't like it when they die. They make tunnels in the ground, and then they eat up Papa's bulbs. And they teach their children to make tunnels and eat bulbs. And at night they all sleep with their arms around each other. They don't know they're unfortunate creatures. Is that a good word?"

"Excellent," said Grandmother, writing as fast as she could.

"And then they get poison corn, or else they get their hind legs caught in a trap. That's good that they get caught, or their stomachs get poisoned and explode! But what are we supposed to do? Write: What are we supposed to do, since we can't ever punish them until they've already done something, and then it's too late, anyway. It's a hard problem. They have more children every twenty minutes."

"Every twenty days," Grandmother muttered.

"And they teach their children. Not just field mice—all the little animals that teach their children. And there get to be more and more of them, and they all teach their children, and so they're all brought up wrong. And the worst ones are the ones that are so small they're all over the place, and you don't see them till you've already stepped on them. And sometimes you don't even see them then, but you know, so you have a bad conscience anyway. Whatever you do, it's just as bad, and so the best thing is not to do anything at all, or else think about something else. The End. Is there enough room for an illustration?"

"Yes," Grandmother said.

"You draw it," Sophia said. "How does it all sound?"

"Shall I read it?"

"No," Sophia said. "No, I don't think so. I don't have time right now. But you can save it for my children."

Sophia's Storm

THERE WAS ONE SUMMER that was never referred to by year, but only as the summer of the great storm. Not in human memory had such huge waves swept through the Gulf of Finland from the east. The winds reached fifty, but the waves rose to a height and length that indicated sixty, or, some people insisted, seventy knots. It happened on a weekend when the radio had predicted gentle, variable winds, so boats were all rigged for good weather. That any of them escaped must be ascribed to God's mercy, for the storm came up in half an hour and built swiftly to its full intensity. Afterward, government helicopters flew along the coast and plucked up people clinging to rocks or the bottoms of their swamped boats. The helicopters landed on every skerry where there was any trace of life, or the simplest building, and very carefully put down the name of the island and the names of the survivors on a list. If only people had known from the outset that everyone would be saved, they could have given the storm their full attention and admiration. For years afterward, coastal people never met without talking about the storm, where they had been that day, and what they had done when the storm came up.

The day started out warm, wrapped in a yellowish haze, and long swells moved through the sea in barely perceptible surges. Later, there was a great deal of talk about the yellow haze and the swell, and many people were reminded of the typhoons in their childhood sea stories. In addition, the water was unusually shiny, and much lower than normal.

Grandmother packed fruit juice and sandwiches in a basket, and the family reached North Grayskerry at about noon. Sophia's father set out two nets west of the island, and Grandmother rowed for him. North Grayskerry always seemed terribly forlorn and melancholy, but they could never resist

going there. The abandoned pilots' cottage was long
and low. Its stone foundation had been built by the
Russians and was fastened to the rock with iron
cramps. The roof had fallen in on one side, but the
little square tower in the middle was undamaged.
Hundreds of swallows darted around the house,
whistling shrilly. The door was secured with a big
rusty padlock, and the key was not hanging beside
the door. The steps were surrounded by a wall of
nettles.

Papa sat down near the water to work. It was
very warm. The swell had grown heavier, and the
strong yellow light over the water hurt his eyes. He
leaned back against a rock and fell asleep.

"It feels like a thunderstorm," Grandmother
said. "And the well stinks worse than ever."

"It's full of crap," Sophia said.

They peered down into the narrow hole of the
well, through all the rings of cement down into the
darkness. They always smelled the well. Then they
inspected the pilots' garbage heap.

"Where's your father?"

"He's asleep."

"That's a good idea," Grandmother said. "Wake
me up if you do anything that's fun." She found a
patch of sand among the juniper bushes.

"When are we going to eat? When are we going to go swimming?" Sophia said. "When are we

going to walk around the island? Do we get to eat and go swimming, or don't you ever do anything but sleep?"

It was hot and quiet and lonely. The house was crouched like a long, squat animal, and the black swallows circled above it with piercing shrieks, like knives in the air. Sophia walked all around the shoreline until she was back where she started. On the whole island, there was nothing but rock and juniper and smooth round stones and sand and tufts of dry grass. The sky and the sea were veiled by the yellow haze, which was stronger than sunshine and hurt the eyes. The waves heaved in toward land like hills and curled into breakers at the shore. It was a very heavy swell. "Dear God, let something happen," Sophia prayed. "God, if You love me. I'm bored to death. Amen."

Perhaps the change began when the swallows went silent. The shimmering sky was suddenly empty, and there were no more birds. Sophia waited. The answer to her prayers was in the air. She looked out to sea and saw the horizon turn black. The blackness spread, and the water shivered in dread and expectation. It came closer. The wind reached the island in a high, sighing whisper and swept on by. It was quiet again. Sophia stood waiting on the shore, where the grass lay stretched on the ground like a light-colored pelt. And now a new darkness came sweeping over the water—the great storm itself! She ran toward it and was embraced by the wind. She was cold and fiery at the same time, and she shouted loudly, "It's the wind! It's the wind!" God had sent her a storm of her own. In His immense benevolence, He thrust huge masses of water in toward land, and they rose above the rocky shore and the grass and the moss and roared in among the junipers, and Sophia's hard summer feet thumped across the ground as she ran back and forth praising God! The world was quick and sharp again. Finally, something was happening.

Papa woke up and remembered his nets. The boat lay bumping broadside to the shore, the oars were clattering back and forth, and the motor was digging into the twisted mat of sea grass. He untied the line and pushed out against the waves and started rowing. Mountainous waves angled around the lee shore, while over his head the sky was still yellow and bright and empty, and there sat God and granted Sophia her storm, and all along the coast there was the same confusion and surprise.

Sound asleep, Grandmother felt the rumble of the breakers resounding through the rock, and she sat up and cocked an ear toward the sea.

Sophia threw herself down on her back in the sand beside her and shouted, "It's my storm! I prayed to God for a storm and here it is!"

"Wonderful," Grandmother said. "But the nets are out."

It's never easy to take up a net alone, and in the wind it is nearly impossible. Papa put the motor on slow and headed into the wind and started hauling in. He saved the first net with only one rip, but the second was caught on the bottom. He put the motor on idle and tried to pull it from the side. The line on the edge of the net broke. Finally, he gave up trying to ease it free and simply hauled, and the net came up in a tangled snarl of seaweed and fish, and he heaved it into the bottom of the boat. Sophia and Grandmother stood and watched as the boat approached the shore in overwhelming seas. Papa leaped out and grabbed one side of the boat and pulled, a broad storm wave washed around the point and smacked into the stern and pushed, and when the water swept back out again, the boat was firmly ashore. Papa made it fast, picked up the nets in his arms, and walked toward the house, leaning into the wind. The other two followed along behind him, side by side. Their eyes burned and their lips tasted salty. Grandmother walked with her legs wide apart and planted her walking stick firmly in the ground with each step. The wind stirred up the rubbish by the well and blew it toward them. Everything that had settled down to rot and turn to soil in a hundred years rose up and whirled out over the shore and

into the storming sea: the pilots' old garbage and
the stink from the well and the slow sadness of a
great many summers. The whole island was washed
clean by breakers and flying white foam.

"Do you like it?" Sophia shouted. "It's my
storm! Say you're having fun!"

"Lots of fun," said Grandmother, blinking the
salt water out of her eyes.

Papa threw down the nets by the steps, where
the nettles had blown down into a gray rug, and
then he hurried out alone toward the point to have
a look at the waves. He was in a great rush. Grandmother sat down on the ground and started picking
fish out of the net. Her nose was running and her
hair was flying in all directions.

"It's funny about me," Sophia said. "I always
feel like such a nice girl whenever there's a storm."

"You do?" Grandmother said. "Well, may-
be . . ." Nice, she thought. No. *I'm* certainly not
nice. The best you could say of me is that I'm interested. She extracted a perch and bashed its head
against the rock.

Papa broke the padlock on the door with a big
stone. He did it to save his family.

The front hall was a narrow, dark corridor that
divided the house into two rooms. On the floor were
some dead birds that had been lying there for years,
birds that had entered the disintegrating house and

never found their way out. There was a smell of
rubbish and salt fish. From inside, the constant
sound of the storm changed; it had a threatening
undertone, and seemed closer. They went into the
room on the west side, which still had its roof. It
was quite a small room, with two naked iron beds, a
white stove with a hood, and a table and two chairs
in the middle of the floor. The wallpaper was very
pretty. Papa put their basket on the table and they
drank juice and ate sandwiches. Then he went back
to his work, and Grandmother sat down on the floor
and started picking fish out of the net again. The
walls of the house trembled steadily with the thun-
dering of the sea, and it began to get cold. Spume
from the breakers covered the windowpanes and ran
over the sill and across the floor. Every now and
then Papa would get up and go out to see to the
boat.

The seas breaking against the sheer outer side
of the island had grown. One after the other, the
waves rose up in their white immensity to a tre-
mendous height, and foam hissed against the rocks
like the blows of a whip. Tall curtains of water flew
across the island and sailed on west. The storm was
titanic! Papa fixed another line to the boat, and
when he came back in, he went up to the attic to
look for fuel. The stove was somewhat obstinate,
but when it finally caught, the fire burned with a

furious draft. They stopped being cold even before
the room was warm. Papa put a herring net on the
floor in front of the stove for anyone who wanted to
sleep, and the net was so old it crumbled in his
hands. Finally, he lit his pipe, sat down at the table,
and went back to his work.

Sophia climbed up into the tower. The tower
room was very small and had four windows, one for
each point of the compass. She saw that the island
had shrunk and grown terribly small, nothing but
an insignificant patch of rocks and colorless earth.
But the sea was immense: white and yellow and
gray and horizonless. There was only this one island, surrounded by water, threatened and sheltered
by the storm, forgotten by everyone but God, who
granted prayers. "Oh, God," said Sophia solemnly,
"I didn't realize I was so important. It was awfully
nice of You. Thank You very much. Amen."

Evening came on and the sun turned everything
crimson as it went down. The fire burned in the
stove. The west window glowed red, which made
the wallpaper even prettier. It was torn and spotted,
but now the whole pattern was visible—light blue
and pink, with carefully painted vines. Grandmother cooked fish in a tin can. Luckily enough, she
had found some salt. When he was done eating,
Papa went out to see to his boat.

"I'm not going to sleep all night," Sophia said.

"Think how awful if we'd been home when it started, instead of out here!"

"Well, I suppose," Grandmother said. "But I'm a little worried about the dory. And I can't remember if we closed the window."

"The dory," Sophia whispered.

"Yes, and the cold frames. And we never did stake the gladiolas. And I left some pots soaking in the bay."

"Don't say any more," Sophia shouted.

But Grandmother continued on thoughtlessly. "And then I keep thinking about all the people out at sea . . . And all the boats that will be wrecked."

Sophia stared at her and screamed, "How can you talk like that when you know it's my fault? I prayed for a storm, and it came!" She started crying out loud as a caravan of dreadful, incriminating visions passed before her eyes: broken boats and gladiolas, windows and people, pots and pans rolling about on the bottom of the ocean, and flags shredded by the wind! Oh, God! She saw everything shattered and destroyed.

"I think we did pull up the dory, anyway," Grandmother said.

But Sophia wrapped her arms around her head and wept beneath the weight of the catastrophe that had struck all Eastern Nyland.

"It wasn't your fault," her grandmother said. "Listen to me. There would have been a storm in any case."

"But not as big!" Sophia wept. "It was God and I who did it!"

The sun had gone down, and the room became suddenly dark. The fire was still burning in the stove. And the wind had not let up.

"God and you," Grandmother repeated angrily. "Why should He listen to you, especially, when maybe ten other people prayed for nice weather? And they did, you can count on that."

"But I prayed first," Sophia said. "And you can see for yourself they didn't get nice weather!"

"God," Grandmother said. "God has so much to do, He doesn't have time to listen . . ."

Papa came back and put more wood on the fire. He gave them an old blanket that smelled bad and went out again to look at the waves before it got completely dark.

"You said yourself that He listens," said Sophia coldly. "You said He hears everything you pray for."

Grandmother lay down on the herring net and said, "Yes, He does. But you see I was first."

"What do you mean?"

"I prayed for a storm before you did, that's what."

"When did you pray?" asked Sophia suspiciously.

"This morning."

"But then why," Sophia burst out sternly, "why did you take along so little food and not enough clothes? Didn't you trust Him?"

"Yes, of course . . . But maybe I thought it would be exciting to try and get along without . . ."

Sophia sighed. "Yes," she said. "That's just like you. Did you take your medicine?"

"Yes, I did."

"Good. Then you can go to sleep and stop worrying about all the trouble you've caused. I won't tell anyone."

"That's nice of you," Grandmother said.

The next day at about three o'clock, the wind let up enough for them to get home. The dory lay upside down in front of the veranda, with its duckboards, oars, and bailing bucket all intact. And they had closed the window. There were a number of things God had not had time to save, because Grandmother asked Him too late, but when the wind changed He did roll the pots and pans back up onshore again. And the helicopter came, as they had hoped, and put down their names and the name of the island on a list.

Day of Danger

ONE VERY HOT DAY about noon, the midges started dancing above the tallest spruce tree on the island. Midges—not to be confused with mosquitoes—dance in vertical clouds and always in tempo. Millions and billions of microscopic midges rise and fall in perfect precision, singing stridently.

"The wedding dance," Grandmother said, trying to look up without losing her balance. "My grandmother always used to say you had to be careful when the midges were dancing and the moon was full."

"How come?" Sophia said.

"It's the great mating day, and nothing's safe. You have to be very careful about tempting fate. You mustn't spill salt, or break a mirror, and if the swallows leave your house, you'd better move before sundown. It's all a terrible nuisance."

"Where did your grandmother ever get such dumb ideas?" asked Sophia in disbelief.

"Grandmother was superstitious."

"What's 'superstitious'?"

Grandmother thought for a moment, and then she said that superstitious was when you didn't try to explain things that couldn't be explained. Like, for example, cooking up magic potions when there was a full moon and actually getting them to work. Grandmother's grandmother had been married to a priest, who didn't believe in superstition. Every time he was sick or depressed, his wife would cook up an elixir for him, but the poor woman was forced to do it in secret. And when it made him well, she had to pretend it was Innosemtseff's Tonic that had done the trick. It was a great strain on her over the years.

Sophia and Grandmother sat down by the shore to discuss the matter further. It was a pretty day, and the sea was running a long, windless swell. It was on days just like this—dog days—that boats went sailing off all by themselves. Large, alien objects made their way in from the sea, certain things sank and others rose, milk soured, and dragonflies danced in desperation. Lizards were not afraid. When the moon came up, red spiders mated on uninhabited skerries, where the rock became an unbroken carpet of tiny, ecstatic spiders.

"Maybe we ought to warn Papa," Sophia said.

"I don't think he's superstitious," Grandmother said. "For that matter, superstition is old-fashioned, and you should always believe your father."

"Of course," Sophia said.

The swell carried in a big crown of twisted branches, as if some gigantic animal were wandering slowly in along the ocean floor. The air above the rock stood still and quivered with the heat.

"Didn't your grandmother ever get scared?" Sophia said.

"No, but she liked to scare other people. She'd come in to breakfast and say that now someone was going to die before the moon set, because the knives were crossed in the drawer. Or she would have had a dream about black birds."

"I dreamed about a guinea pig last night," Sophia said. "Do you promise to be careful and not break any bones before the moon sets?"

Grandmother promised.

The odd thing was that the milk actually did go sour. They caught a stickleback in their net. A black butterfly flew into the house and lit on a mirror. And along toward evening Sophia discovered that the knife and the pen on Papa's desk were crossed. She moved them apart as quickly as she could, but of course the damage was done. She ran to the guest room and banged on the door with both hands, and Grandmother opened it right away.

"Something's happened," Sophia whispered. "The knife and the pen were crossed on Papa's desk. No, nothing you say can make it any better!"

"But don't you understand?" Grandmother said.

"My grandmother was just superstitious. She made things up because she was bored, and so that she could tyrannize her family . . ."

"Quiet," said Sophia seriously. "Don't say anything. Don't say anything to me." She left the door standing open and walked away.

The first cool of the evening arrived, and the dancing midges disappeared. The frogs came out and started singing to each other, while the dragon-flies seemed to be dead. In the sky, the last red clouds sank into the yellow ones, making orange. The forest was full of signs and portents, its own secret written language. But what good did that do Papa? There were footprints where no one could have stepped, crossed branches, one red blueberry bush in the midst of all the green ones. The full moon rose and balanced on the top of a juniper bush. Now was the time for unmanned boats to glide out from their shores. Huge, mysterious fish made rings on the water, and the red spiders gathered wherever it was they had decided to meet. Implacable fate sat waiting just over the horizon. Sophia searched for herbs to make an elixir for her father, but all she could find were plain, ordinary plants. It is never clear which plants can be considered herbs. They are very small, presumably, with soft, pale stems. If possible, they should be slightly moldy and grow in swampy places. But how could you tell for sure? The moon rose higher and began its inevitable orbit.

Sophia shouted through the door: "What kind of herbs did she cook, that grandmother of yours?"

"I've forgotten," Grandmother said.

Sophia came in. "Forgotten?" she said between her teeth. "Forgotten? How can you forget a thing like that? If you've forgotten, then what am I supposed to do? How do you expect me to save him before the moon sets?"

Grandmother put aside her book and took off her glasses.

"I've turned superstitious," Sophia said. "I'm even more superstitious than your grandmother was. Do something!"

Grandmother got up and started putting on her clothes.

"Forget the stockings," said Sophia impatiently. "And the corset, too. We have to hurry!"

"But even if we pick the herbs," Grandmother said, "even if we pick them and make an elixir, he won't drink it."

"That's true," Sophia admitted. "Maybe we could pour it in his ear."

Grandmother pulled on her boots while she thought.

Suddenly Sophia started to cry. She had seen the moon over the sea, and a person never knew about the moon. It can set all at once, on its own peculiar schedule. Grandmother opened the door and said, "Now you mustn't say a word. You mustn't sneeze or cry or belch, not even once, until we've gathered everything we need. Then we'll put it all in the safest place we can find and let it work from a distance. In this case, that will be very effective."

The island was bright in the moonlight, and the night was quite warm. Sophia watched as Grandmother plucked the head of a beach pea, picked up two small pebbles and a wisp of dry beach grass, and stuffed it all in her pocket. They walked on. In the woods, Grandmother collected a bit of tree moss, a piece of fern, and a dead moth. Sophia followed along silently, her nerves growing a little calmer with each item that Grandmother put in her pocket. The moon looked slightly red and was almost as bright as day. A path of moonlight led toward them over the water, all the way to the shore. They went straight across the island to the other side, and now and then Grandmother would bend over to pick some important ingredient. Large and black, she moved along in the path of the moon. Her stiff legs and her walking stick marched steadily forward, and she grew larger and larger. The moonlight rested on her hat and her shoulders as she watched over fate and the island. There was not the least doubt but what she would find what they needed to avert misfortune and death. It all found a place in her pocket. Sophia followed along right behind her and saw how Grandmother carried the moon on her head, and the night became utterly serene. When they were back at the house, Grandmother said they could talk again.

"Quiet!" Sophia whispered. "Don't talk. Let it lie there in your pocket."

"Good," Grandmother said. She broke off a little piece of rotting wood from the steps and put it in with the rest, and then she went to bed. The moon sank into the sea, and there was no cause for alarm.

From that day on, Grandmother kept her cigarettes and matches in her left-hand pocket, and they all lived together happily until fall. Then Grandmother sent her coat to the cleaners, and almost immediately Sophia's father sprained his ankle.

August

EVERY YEAR, the bright Scandinavian summer nights fade away without anyone's noticing. One evening in August you have an errand outdoors, and all of a sudden it's pitch-black. A great warm, dark silence surrounds the house. It is still summer, but the summer is no longer alive. It has come to a standstill; nothing withers, and fall is not ready to begin. There are no stars yet, just darkness. The can of kerosene is brought up from the cellar and left in the hall, and the flashlight is hung up on its peg beside the door.

Not right away, but little by little and incidentally, things begin to shift position in order to follow the progress of the seasons. Day by day, everything moves closer to the house. Sophia's father takes in the tent and the water pump. He removes the buoy and attaches the cable to a cork float. The boat is pulled ashore on a cradle, and the dory is hung upside down behind the woodyard. And so fall begins. A few days later, they dig the potatoes and roll the water barrel up against the wall of the house. Buckets and garden tools move in toward the house, ornamental pots disappear, Grandmother's parasol and other transitory and attractive objects all change places. The fire extinguisher and the axe, the pick and the snow shovel, appear on the veranda. And at the same time, the whole landscape is transformed.

Grandmother had always liked this great change in August, most of all, perhaps, because of the way it never varied: a place for everything and everything in its place. Now was the time for the traces of habitation to disappear, and, as far as possible, for the island to return to its original condition. The exhausted flower beds were covered with banks of seaweed. The long rains did their leveling and rinsing. All the flowers still in bloom were either red or yellow, strong patches of color above the seaweed. In the woods were a few enormous white roses that blossomed and lived for one day in breathless splendor.

Grandmother's legs ached, which may have been due to the rain, and she couldn't walk around the island as much as she wanted to. But she went out for a little while every day just before dark, and tidied up the ground. She picked up everything that had to do with human beings. She gathered nails and bits of paper and cloth and plastic, pieces of lumber covered with oilspill, and an occasional bottle top. She went down to the shore and built fires where everything burnable could go right ahead and burn, and all the time she felt the island growing cleaner and cleaner, and more and more foreign and distant. It's shaking us off, she thought. It will soon be uninhabited. Almost.

The nights got darker and darker. There was an unbroken chain of navigational lights and beacons along the horizon, and sometimes big boats thumped by in the channel. The sea was motionless.

When the ground was clean, Sophia's father

painted all the ringbolts with red lead, and one warm, rainless day he soaked the veranda with seal fat. He oiled the tools and the hinges, and swept the chimney. He put away the nets. He stacked wood against the wall by the stove for next spring, and for anyone who might be shipwrecked on the island, and he tied down the woodshed with ropes because it stood so near the high-water mark.

"We have to take in the flower stakes," Grandmother said. "They spoil the landscape." But Sophia's father let them be, for otherwise he wouldn't know what was there in the ground when they came back. Grandmother worried about a lot of things. "Suppose someone lands here," she said. "They always do. They wouldn't know the coarse salt is in the cellar, and the trapdoor may have swelled from the damp. We have to bring up the salt and label it, so they won't think it's sugar. And we ought to put out some more pants—there's nothing worse than wet pants. What if they hang their nets over the flower bed and trample it all down? You never know about roots." A little later, she started worrying about the stovepipe and put up a sign: "Don't close the damper. It might rust shut. If it doesn't draw, there may be a bird's nest in the chimney—later on in the spring, that is."

"But we'll be back by then," Sophia's father said.

"You never know about birds," Grandmother said. She took down the curtains a week early and covered the south and east windows with disposable paper bedsheets, on which she wrote, "Don't remove the window covers or the fall birds will try to fly right through the house. Use anything you need, but please carry in some more wood. There are tools under the workbench. Enjoy yourselves."

"Why are you in such a rush?" Sophia asked, and her grandmother answered that it was a good idea to do things before you forgot that they had to be done. She set out cigarettes and candles, in case the lamp didn't work, and she hid the barometer, the sleeping bags, and the seashell box under the bed. Later, she brought out the barometer again. She never hid the figurine. Grandmother knew no one understood sculpture, and she thought it wouldn't hurt them to be exposed to a little culture. She also made Papa leave the rugs on the floor, so the room wouldn't look unfriendly over the winter.

Covering two of the windows changed the room, made it secretive and conspiratorial, and, at the same time, very lonely.

Grandmother polished the handle on the door and scoured the garbage pail. The next day, she washed all her clothes out beside the woodyard. Then she was tired and went to the guest room. The guest room grew very crowded with the

approach of fall—it was a good place to put all sorts
of things that were waiting for spring or were
no longer needed. Grandmother liked being surrounded by practical, commonplace things, and before she went to sleep, she studied everything
around her: nets, nail kegs, coils of steel wire and
rope, sacks full of peat, and other important items.
With an odd kind of tenderness, she examined the
nameplates of boats long since broken up, some
storm indications that had been written on the wall,
penciled data on dead seals they had found and a
mink they had shot, and she dwelled particularly on
the pretty picture of the hermit in his open tent
against a sea of desert sand, with his guardian lion
in the background. How can I ever leave this room?
she thought.

It wasn't easy to get into the room and take her
clothes off and open the window for the night air,
but finally she could lie down and stretch her legs.
She blew out the light and listened to Sophia and
her father getting ready for bed on the other side of
the wall. There was a smell of tar and wet wool and
maybe a trace of turpentine, and the sea was still
quiet. As Grandmother fell asleep, she remembered
the chamberpot under the bed and how much she
hated it, this symbol of helplessness. She had ac-
cepted it out of pure politeness. A chamberpot is
nice to have when it's storming or raining, but the

next day you have to carry it clear down to the water, and anything that has to be hidden is a burden.

When she woke up, she lay for a long time and wondered if she should go out or not. It felt as if the night had come right up to the walls and was waiting outside, and her legs ached. The stairs were badly constructed. The steps were too high and too narrow, and then came the rock, which was slippery down toward the woodyard, and then you had to come all the way back again. No sense in lighting a light; it only makes you lose your sense of direction and distance, and the darkness comes closer. Swing your legs over the edge of the bed and wait for your balance to come right. Four steps to the door and open the latch and wait again, then five steps down, holding the handrail. Grandmother wasn't afraid of falling or losing her way, but she knew the darkness was absolute, and she knew what it was like when you lose your hold and there's nothing left to go by. All the same, she said to herself, I know perfectly well what everything looks like. I don't have to see it. She swung her legs over the edge of the bed and waited for a moment. She took the four careful steps to the door and opened the latch. The night was black, but no longer so warm; there was a fine, sharp chill. She went down the stairs very slowly, turned away from the house,

and let go of the railing. It wasn't as hard as she'd
expected. As she crouched in the woodyard, she
knew exactly where she was, and where the house
and the sea and the woods were. From far off in the
channel came the thump of a boat sailing past, but
she couldn't see the channel lights.

Grandmother sat down on the chopping stump
to wait for her balance. It came quickly, but she
stayed where she was. The coastal freighter was
headed east to Kotka. The sound of its diesel motors
gradually died, and the night was as quiet as before.
It smelled of fall. A new boat approached, a small
boat, probably running on gasoline. It might be a
herring boat with an automobile engine—but not
this late at night. They always went out right after
sunset. In any case, it wasn't in the channel but
heading straight out to sea. Its slow thumping
passed the island and continued out, farther and
farther away, but never stopping.

"Isn't that funny," Grandmother said. "It's only
my heart, it's not a herring boat at all." For a long
time she wondered if she should go back to bed or
stay where she was. She guessed she would stay for
a while.

About the Author

TOVE JANSSON is a Finnish writer and painter, who lives, during half the year, on an island off the coast of Finland. Although she has written several books for adults, she is best known in the United States for her children's stories, the Moomin books, for which she was awarded the Hans Christian Andersen Children's Book Medal in 1966.